The killer hauled Zoe in front of him and lifted his weapon.

She stared down the barrel, and a sob caught in her throat. "I didn't see anything." Okay, that was a lie, but it was the first thing that had come to mind. "The lady looked dead. He was standing over her, and I assumed he killed her. I could be mistaken."

She wanted to laugh through the sob. She was going crazy, seconds before she was going to die.

The killer grinned, more of a sneer. "Wrong place, seriously wrong time. And you just couldn't let it lie. Well, turns out neither can they."

"I won't say anything. I promise."

"Too late. You've drawn attention to yourself. Now they're convinced you'll blab, and that can't happen. So instead of taking you to them, I'm ending this. No more scare tactics. No more threats. Problem solved."

Them? Realization dawned on her that he was going to kill her, and she moved. As fast as she could. Everything in her screamed to *run.*

He pulled the trigger.

Lisa Phillips is a British-born tea-drinking, guitar-playing wife and mom of two. She and her husband lead worship together at their local church. Lisa pens high-stakes stories of mayhem and disaster where you can find made-for-each-other love that always ends in a happily-ever-after. She understands that faith is a work in progress more exciting than any story she can dream up. You can find out more about her books at authorlisaphillips.com.

Books by Lisa Phillips

Love Inspired Suspense

Secret Service Agents

Security Detail
Homefront Defenders
Yuletide Suspect
Witness in Hiding

Double Agent
Star Witness
Manhunt
Easy Prey
Sudden Recall
Dead End

WITNESS IN HIDING

LISA PHILLIPS

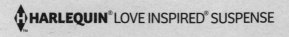

HARLEQUIN® LOVE INSPIRED® SUSPENSE

Recycling programs
for this product may
not exist in your area.

LOVE INSPIRED BOOKS

ISBN-13: 978-1-335-54371-4

Witness in Hiding

Copyright © 2018 by Lisa Phillips

www.Harlequin.com

Printed in U.S.A.

Thou art my hiding place;
thou shalt preserve me from trouble; thou shalt
compass me about with songs of deliverance.
–*Psalms* 32:7

To those who struggle, stand firm and keep fighting.

ONE

Zoe Marks was being followed. That tingle on the back of her neck was constant as she pulled her ball cap low and stepped inside the Laundromat. Had he found her? She'd been so careful, but maybe this was it…the day he finally caught up.

And killed her.

Downtown Salt Lake City was busy just after eleven at night, and she'd hoped to disappear in the crowds. Maybe it hadn't worked.

Moose wasn't behind the counter. The man had been recommended by a mutual contact, and he should be here. He'd said as much at their first meeting.

Moose had a craggy face, the nose that had earned him the moniker and a huge belly that hung over his belt buckle. He didn't exactly blend in. If he was here she'd be able to spot him, but he wasn't out behind the register tonight. Was he waiting in his office?

Zoe made her way down the center aisle, between rows of washers and dryers stacked on either side of the room. The long, low bench in the middle.

A young woman in the corner folded a pair of skinny jeans. Probably two sizes smaller than the ones Zoe wore. Her hair hung over most of her face, and she didn't make eye contact. That was fine with Zoe. Behind the counter an older woman with purple hair sat reading a fashion magazine.

During the three weeks she'd been in hiding, Zoe had learned more than she wanted to about the criminal element. Top of the list was the fact that she had to talk the talk with these people. She couldn't give away anything personal, or emotional. Least of all was the fact that Zoe Marks was an office assistant, a divorcée and the single mom of the most precocious seven-year-old boy in the world. No, she had to be one of them. An anonymous lady who wanted a way out of this life.

Zoe rapped her knuckles on the Formica. "Lookin' for Moose."

The counter woman didn't look up from her magazine.

Zoe pushed aside the depressing thoughts of what her life had become. She couldn't even *think* about Tyler, or she'd start blubbering because she hadn't seen her son in a week—the longest they'd ever been apart. Right now, Tyler was safe with her sister, which meant it wasn't time for crying; it was time for action. The kind that would make the two of them free of danger for the rest of their lives.

Hence, Moose. And the duffel bag of thirty thousand dollars of borrowed money she was going to have to figure out how to pay back.

Freedom wasn't cheap.

The purple-haired woman pointed one white-tipped finger to the interior door. "Moose is back there."

"Thanks." Zoe straightened her shoulders and headed for the back door. Politeness wasn't something the people in this world she'd fallen into understood, but it was ingrained in her. At the last second before she pushed the handle down, another ingrained part of her—some latent warning instinct—flared to life. *Danger.* She glanced back at the front door of the Laundromat just as *he* walked through.

Gun raised, pointed at her.

No life in his eyes.

No emotion in the flat line of his lips.

The woman folding clothes dropped her basket and ran behind him out the door. The gunman made no move to stop her.

Ice-cold terror froze every part of her. It

wasn't Zoe's life that flashed before her eyes—it was Tyler's. Memories raced through her mind of those long-gone happy days. Before Nathan decided he liked his girlfriend better than his wife and moved to New England.

The life Tyler once had was gone now, but he still had her. She wouldn't let him become an orphan today. Her son was everything to her, and there was nothing she wouldn't do to keep him safe. There was no room in her life for anything else—or anyone else. Just her son, who needed his mom alive. It was Zoe's job to make their lives safe.

"Nice try." The gunman smirked.

Zoe couldn't move. All she could do was stare into his evil eyes and wait for death while her mind screamed at her to run. While images of death played across her mind. A woman, lying on the ground. The man stood over her. Her killer.

Now he'd sent this guy to silence her, so she could never tell anyone what she'd seen.

The man twisted, aimed his gun past Zoe. He pulled the trigger over and over again. The woman behind Zoe screamed and hit the floor.

"No loose ends." His voice was as devoid of emotion as his eyes.

Zoe backed up and felt for the door handle. If she didn't try to run he would certainly kill her. She should have bought that gun when she'd had the chance, but she didn't know how to use one. Now she would die because she hadn't been brave enough to overcome a simple fear of the unknown. Dead both because of what she didn't know—how to use a gun—and because of what she did. But Zoe couldn't think about what she'd witnessed. She only wanted to forget it. She never would. Not for the rest of her life.

Her slick fingers slipped off the door handle, but it opened anyway. Zoe didn't know whether to rush through, or just duck.

Moose brushed past her, shotgun in his hands.

Zoe dived out of the way, behind the counter, issuing a quiet apology when she landed on the counter lady's leg. The ball cap flew off Zoe's head, releasing her spray of red curls. The woman was wide-eyed, a red stain on her shoulder.

"What is going—" Moose's roared words cut off. *Bang. Bang.*

Zoe scrambled across the floor. The shotgun went off, then the gunman's weapon—shot after shot. She covered her ears. There was nowhere to go. She was pinned behind the counter with no way out, and that man was coming for her.

Defenseless and innocent. Why did she have to die like a criminal? It was proof God's love for her, His grace, had been withdrawn. For whatever reason, He wasn't on her side anymore. His love and support had been rich during those years with Nathan and Tyler. They'd been together as a family and her life had been good. Now, nothing. God's place in her heart was empty—He'd abandoned her.

Otherwise she wouldn't be about to die on the dirty linoleum floor of a Laundromat.

Secret Service agent Jude Brauer had gone on alert the moment the first shot rang out. He tossed his notebook back on the driver's seat and slammed the car door, palming his weapon instead. Question time would have to come later. There wasn't even time to wait for police backup. He'd seen people inside and heard the gun battle. Jude couldn't let an innocent person die. Seconds counted for everything in situations like this.

The windows of the Laundromat were glass, the lights on inside. His view was crystal clear between the red letters of the store name.

One assailant, center of the room.

A man down, discarded shotgun on the floor. Jude was pretty sure that was Moose, the man he'd been coming to meet. Moose was dead, which meant Jude would never get answers from him now.

The gunman advanced. The second of two women had dived behind the counter. Jude couldn't let anyone else die.

Gun drawn, Jude pushed the front door open with his foot. "Secret Service, put your hands up!"

The guy spun, already firing, not even bothering to aim—but two shots later the clip in his gun emptied. Jude wasn't hit.

Thank You, God.

He put two rounds from his Sig Sauer in the man's chest. He hated to use lethal force, but there was no telling if this man had additional weapons or ammunition. The threat had to be taken out before anyone else was hurt.

The gunman's body jerked as the shots impacted, but he didn't go down. He actually grinned. "Won't work, pig." He said it like he thought he was invincible. High on something? His eyes were glassy, and that bravado had to come from somewhere. It was more than the protective vest he might have under his jacket.

As he stepped closer, Jude wondered if this had to do with his case or something else entirely. The task force he was part of was investigating a local pharmaceutical company with ties to foreign money. Moose might be the key to the whole thing, but it was only a hunch Jude had. He hadn't brought anyone else in case it turned out to be nothing. Now Moose was dead.

The gunman ran to the interior door, where he glanced once behind the counter and said, "See you soon, Zoe."

Then he raced through to whatever back rooms were beyond it.

Jude sprinted after him. He did the same glance maneuver the gunman had and saw a beautiful redhead on the floor, her wide green eyes looking up at him. Jude ordered, "Stay here," to her and the purple-haired woman she lay there with. A woman who'd been shot. "And call an ambulance."

He didn't wait for her to nod; he just ran after the man into a fluorescent-lit hall with bland white walls. Two rooms. The gunman ignored both and hit the exit bar on the door at the end of the hall before he raced out into the night.

The guy had to have been wearing a vest to absorb those shots. Jude wasn't wearing his, not on what should've been a routine inter-view. He had to be careful. This guy wasn't afraid to kill.

And then there was the woman. Zoe, he'd

called her. Who was she, and why did the gunman know her? The man had threatened her, and yet he'd let her live while he killed the man Jude had been there to see.

Had he shot Moose because of the shotgun, or because Moose knew too much? Maybe there was another reason entirely.

Jude reached the exit door, stood where there was cover and looked out before he moved to pursue the man. It wouldn't do him any good to rush out and have the gunman attack him because he hadn't been cautious. But the man wasn't waiting.

The peal of car tires screeched out the parking lot and the killer tore off at top speed in a silver, low-slung, rusty car. No plates. The undercarriage scraped the asphalt on the way out, and then the guy was gone.

Lost him.

Jude slammed the flat of his hand on the door frame. That man—whoever he was and whatever his motive might be—had just killed the best lead Jude had been able to find on his case.

He pulled out his phone and called 9-1-1 to report what had happened.

Jude's job was mostly to identity theft investigations and illegal transactions. White-collar crimes involving money and state-of-the-art technology that cost this country millions each year. Jude would dig into the problem. He would solve the mystery of what was happening and who was involved.

In this particular case, the pharmaceutical company and a South American cartel were moving money back and forth. It hadn't been easy to trace the international transactions. But when Jude had found the Laundromat listed on one, he'd jumped on the information. He didn't have enough evidence to obtain a warrant yet, but that hadn't stopped him from heading over to the Laundromat to see what Moose had to say.

Online banking was the new cash. Huge transfers could be divided up into hundreds of small transactions or transfers between online accounts. It was the job of the Secret Service to recognize evidence of possible money laundering. The question was, who had been sending the pharmaceutical company so much money, and why?

Now his only lead was a rusty car. He'd have to get a description of the vehicle and the gunman to the cops and pray for a result.

Jude trailed back through the hall to a now open door. The other was signed as a bathroom. Before he got there, he glanced around. Security cameras had been installed at the cor-

anything at all. She'd faced enough questions from the injured woman out front.

Before she shoved away Zoe's attempt to help her. Like it was Zoe's fault her shoulder was bleeding.

Cute though this guy was, with dark blond hair in need of a cut curling around his ears, she couldn't trust him. Nice suit. But not too nice; it just fit him really well. She'd always disliked guys who tried too hard to look put-together, or who used styling product in their hair—which was basically the same thing. This guy was clean-cut, and he looked…low-key.

Zoe bit the inside of her cheek. "I should go."

He didn't move, even though she needed to get past him so she could leave this building of horrors empty-handed. *Don't think about that*. But she had to. She needed the reminder of everything that could go wrong to push her to be smart and cautious, to do everything she had to in order to keep her family alive.

This should have been her last stop. Her ticket out for herself, her sister and her son. They would have been on their way. Free.

That was gone now. All she had was nothing but a bag full of cash and no hope.

Not to mention, the police would be here soon.

"How about you stay for a minute. Introduce yourself?" He didn't voice it like a question, even though technically it was. "I'll even start." He touched his chest. "Jude Brauer, Secret Service."

So that was what the badge on his belt signified. Zoe glanced at the wall like she could see outside and said, "Is the president in town?"

He winced. "I'm local, not on the president's detail."

"This is a nice chat and all, but I really should be going." Where, she had no idea. But *anywhere* was fine when it would be away from a dead man, a woman who'd been shot and the end of all her options.

"And you're Zoe."

He wasn't going to listen. He was trying to get her to open up when she had zero intention of doing so. Zoe moved then, and some distant, still hopeful part of her prayed he'd just step aside and let her pass. Like prayer would actually work for her now, when it hadn't so far.

He held out a hand. While not actually touching her, it was still a gentleman's attempt to get her to stay. The fact that he didn't force her to stop resonated in that same distant, hopeful part of her from which she'd just prayed. Zoe didn't let it penetrate. She couldn't, or she'd stop and maybe entertain the idea that this guy might actually be able to help her.

Which he couldn't. No one could.

She stepped past him, into the hallway. "Zoe." His voice was almost kind. She'd been through something traumatic and he adjusted accordingly. His wife probably loved that gentle voice. Zoe chose to ignore it.

She didn't go back to the front of the store. There was nothing but blood and death up there, and the woman who had been shot hadn't wanted her help. Zoe had called for the ambulance, then realized she had to find the ID's Moose had made for her before the cops came. Now she needed to get out of here before they asked too many questions. Before her name ended up on a police record, and her whereabouts were discovered. Anything that could lead to her would do exactly that—and the wrong people would find her.

Zoe moved to the exit door at the end of the hall. Jude Braucr had told her to stay put. *Right.* The last time she'd stayed it had ruined her life. Not again. No way.

"You can't leave, Zoe. You just witnessed a crime. Wait for the cops so you can give your statement."

"I didn't see anything." The words slipped from her mouth and she winced.

"You're going to lie?"

No, she wasn't going to lie. "I can't talk to the cops."

"That guy knew you, and yet he didn't kill you." Jude cocked his head to the side. "Was that because I was here?"

"How am I supposed to know?"

"I'm guessing that you know a whole lot more than you want to admit to me right now."

She didn't say anything, because he was right. Sirens grew in volume. They were right outside. An ambulance. Cops. She couldn't trust the cops. That had been made completely plain to her when she'd tried to report what she'd seen. No one had believed her, and then she and Tyler had been followed. They'd barely escaped.

Zoe had no intention of repeating that frightful afternoon.

Jude turned toward the sound. While his gaze was averted, Zoe slipped out the back door.

Still, part of her almost wanted to stay.

Almost.

TWO

She'd ditched him. Jude could hardly believe she'd actually done it. Slipped out the back door right when his back was turned, leaving him standing in the hallway talking to himself. He sprinted to the door and ran outside. Looked around. She was gone from the areas lit by streetlights. Had she hidden in the shadows?

"Police!" a voice called from the front door. "Anyone here?"

A woman screamed. Not Zoe; it must have been the purple-haired woman from behind the counter. She needed help.

What he wanted to do was search all the dark places out back for Zoe. Instead, Jude announced himself as he strode into the Laundromat, then explained to the responding officers what had happened. An ambulance showed up, and the injured woman was taken to the hospital. Then two suited detectives and a couple of crime scene investigators arrived. Moose's body had to be processed.

He explained again what had happened, but all Jude could think about was those wide green eyes. Terrified. Scared of him, and searching for a way out.

"She just left?"

Jude nodded. "I only turned around for a second and she was gone."

The detectives shared a look.

"She was scared. Jittery. I'm going to search the back parking lot some more. Maybe you can pull feed from the security cameras. Get a picture of her."

"If Moose actually had real cameras instead of fake plastic ones then that might be doable."

Jude sighed. His lead was gone, and so was the woman. Now he was back to square one on who had been sending money to the pharmaceutical company. Or why. He said, "I'm going to look out back."

What he should do was head back to the office and write a report on what he'd tried—and failed—to do. Though he'd rather drive the streets in this area and try to find the woman. He'd probably never see her again.

Why that bothered him Jude didn't want to think about. She was probably a criminal involved in a deal with Moose, walking the darker side of the law.

The detectives shook his hand. One said, "We'll call if we need anything."

Jude nodded and headed to the door, his thoughts still on Zoe. The fear in her eyes had been real. She'd been scared. Frustrated she couldn't find whatever she was looking for. Had she stuck around, Jude might have been able to find out more about her. If she needed help, she should have asked him for it.

Jude clicked the locks on his car and realized he'd left it unlocked when he heard the gunshots. Thankfully no one had stolen it while he was inside. Couldn't be too careful in this part of town. He slid in behind the wheel, ruminating about the case.

Everything about it smelled of a powerful broker who needed…something from the Salt Lake City–based pharmaceutical company. Money laundering, but why had they used this approach? Surely there were easier ways to do it than using the many accounts held by such a high-profile company.

As Jude drove in the general direction of the office, his phone rang. He touched the display screen, and said, "Agent Brauer."

"Jude, honey. It's Mrs. McAffrey."

"Is something wrong with you or Turner?"

Mrs. McAffrey was his eighty-six-year-old neighbor, the widow of a Salt Lake City police officer.

Turner was Jude's dog, who she kept an eye on. He figured she left the gate between their yards open because she wanted the company of his old mutt. She also gave him so many treats, and scraps of chicken, Jude hardly needed to feed him.

"No, honey." She used the endearment like it was going out of style. "He was out barking at the squirrels an hour ago, but it's all quiet now."

"Oh, good. What can I help you with?"

"Well, see, the water in my bathroom sink won't shut off. I've turned and turned the knob but it just keeps streaming out." She paused, and then in her hopeful voice said, "Could you come look at it, honey?"

"I'm at work right now, but I can call a plumber for you." He knew she didn't sleep much, but had she looked at the time?

"And have some stranger traipsing through my house?" There it was, her hopeful voice again.

Jude ground his teeth, but heard a noise in his backseat. It didn't sound like any of the debris rolling around back there. Instead, it almost sounded like a giggle. He glanced in the rearview, but couldn't see anything. He needed to keep his eyes on the road, not lower the mirror's angle. He made a right-hand turn instead of getting on the freeway, and headed for a store parking lot.

He explained to Mrs. McAffrey how to shut off the water using the valve in the cupboard under the sink.

"It's very tight. I'm not sure…" She went quiet for a second. "I did it!"

"Good," he said. Half his attention was on the backseat, but he didn't hear anything else from that direction. "It's still broken, but at least you're not leaking water anymore. I'll come by first thing in the morning and check it out." Hopefully it would be an easy problem, like a worn-down washer.

"Thank you, honey."

"No problem, Mrs. McAffrey." Jude hung up and pulled into a parking space. He got out of the car and drew his weapon, stepped to the back door and yanked it open.

The redhead with green eyes sat in the foot well behind the driver's seat, one hand over her mouth as tears streamed down her face. Zoe took a breath, let go of her mouth and burst out laughing. "That was hilarious. That old woman totally bamboozled you." She seemed on the verge of hysterics.

"Get out of my car."

Even though she was laughing uncontrollably and tears still rolled down her face, she shook her head. She clambered onto the backseat and shifted away from him at the same time, the duffel over one shoulder so that it bunched against the backrest and lifted her elbow that lay on it.

"Don't get out the other side." If she ran again, he'd have to chase her.

She leaned forward. That was the moment Jude knew she'd completely lost it. The hysterical laughing turned to hysterical crying and lasted long enough for Jude to child lock the rear doors on both sides before shutting her in. Then he got back in the front seat and pulled the wad of coffee house napkins from the glove box. "Here."

She looked at him. She was still pretty, but this might be what his sister called ugly crying. He didn't put his weapon away, but he did wait until she had pulled herself together before he said, "Why are you in my car?"

Zoe shook her head. Her hair snagged under the strap of the duffel on her shoulder and… shifted. Jude blinked before he realized what was happening. "You're wearing a wig?"

She blew out a breath and pulled the long, gorgeous red hair from her head. Shame. Still, the dark hair pinned against her head wasn't unappealing. Those eyes though…

Wait. Was she wearing colored contacts? Maybe everything that drew him to her was fake. Jude's stomach churned at the idea he'd been duped. This beautiful, innocent-seeming woman was clearly a fraud. He'd been right to be suspicious, and now he was harboring a criminal.

"What do you want, Zoe? Or is that even your real name?" He didn't like the hard edge to his voice, but what did she expect after she lied to him? At least she had the decency to wince. Jude was out of patience. "Either start talking or get out." A thought occurred to him. "You ran out of the Laundromat. You left. You could have gotten away clean. Why are you in my car? And how did you get in it without being seen, since those cops pulled up right beside it?"

"They were inside," she said. "They didn't see me, and neither did anyone else." Why did it seem like she didn't know if that was good or bad?

"You should've stayed and talked to the cops. They need your statement."

She shook her head then, and a fresh tear rolled down her face. "I can't talk to the cops."

"You witnessed a crime."

"That doesn't mean I have to testify. They can't make me if I don't want to tell them anything."

Jude frowned. Why was she in his car if she didn't want to talk to the cops? He was law enforcement. "Sure, they can't force you to say anything, but isn't the right thing to tell them what you know? It could help catch that guy."

Her gaze flicked away.

"He knew you." When she didn't say anything, Jude said, "He used your name."

He had. And this man, Secret Service agent Jude Brauer, had heard it. When she'd run out the back door she'd only gone two steps before she ducked to the side and hid behind the Dumpster. If movies were to be trusted, Jude would run past her, expecting her to be ahead of him. Hardly anyone thought to check right where the chase started.

And so she'd hidden, the same way she'd been hiding for three weeks now—right under their noses.

Zoe should be miles away by now, but she was out of options. Her final plan—the fake passports Moose had made—was out of reach now. Zoe had no one to turn to. She was out of ideas.

Enter Jude Brauer.

For whatever reason she didn't much want to ponder, Zoe had crept from that hiding spot and around the building to the imposing car with government plates. He'd looked at her with so much compassion, and she hadn't been ready to let that go.

As soon as the coast had been clear, she'd booked it across the lot, not really sure what she'd been expecting to do. And then she thanked God a million times his car had been unlocked. She'd been able to hide. God might not like her right now, but she knew when thanks were due.

His car. That phone call. For a few minutes everything she'd been through had washed away and she'd actually felt...safe.

He held out his hand from the front seat of his SUV. Zoe stared at it. She wasn't agreeing to anything; she wasn't trusting him, but she had to do *something*.

So she put her hand in his. Strong, warm fingers closed around hers. His eyes glowed with approval. Attraction wasn't something she could deal with right now, so she pushed the feeling aside. Safety meant so much more.

"It's nice to meet you, Zoe. I'm Jude."

"Hi, Jude."

He let go, but the feeling didn't dissipate. Inside this car she actually felt safe. It was so foreign she almost didn't recognize it. Some part of her had seen him in that hallway and just...*known*. Either way, she knew she'd done the right thing.

It didn't mean she was trusting him, but Zoe had to face the fact that she seriously needed help. Moose was dead. That guy, the one who had been chasing her for three weeks, so close she'd almost been able to feel his breath hot on her neck...he'd shot Moose and let her live. He must have been given orders to keep her alive, but why? Silencing her would mean the truth died with her. She had nothing but questions—and no way to find answers.

Echoing her thoughts, Jude asked, "So, what now?"

Zoe shook her head. "I have no idea."

"Why do I think you don't just mean you have no idea where we should go right now?" His lips curled into a smile. "Maybe I meant coffee, or dinner."

Zoe set her hand over her queasy stomach as the image of Moose falling to the floor played through her mind. "I don't think I'm going to eat for a week after that."

"I know what you mean." His face turned grim.

"Is that woman okay?"

Jude nodded. "We do need to talk. You're

obviously in trouble, or you need help. I'd like to know why."

"I didn't do anything wrong!" The words burst from her lips, the need to defend herself as strong as it always had been.

"I'm not saying you did. What I meant was, why would you turn to *me*?"

"You were there."

He waited. Then said, "And?"

Zoe shrugged. It wasn't the connection. There was one, but that wasn't it. She hadn't known before she got in the car that being in here with Jude Brauer would feel so…safe.

"You have to talk, Zoe. You have to tell me something so I know how to help you."

"What about getting back to work? That's the excuse you gave Mrs. McAffrey."

"It wasn't an excuse. I *am* working—it's why I was at the Laundromat. To talk with Moose."

Her arm on the duffel bag tightened on a reflex. Jude's glance went to it, not missing a single thing. Why couldn't she have been better at this cloak-and-dagger, superspy stuff?

Zoe sighed. "That's why I can't talk to the cops. They'll think I had something to do with Moose's business." Technically, they wouldn't be wrong. No, she wasn't a regular customer. She didn't know, or want to know, who his usual customers were. But she had hired his services. If Jude wanted to question her about Moose, she wouldn't have anything to tell him. She hadn't transacted anything with Moose before he died. The introduction had been conducted through a third party, and today was only the second time she'd even seen the man.

Jude studied her. *Great.* He probably thought she was a criminal. "How did that shooter know you?"

Zoe measured her words. "I've seen him before, several times over the past three weeks. Usually just out the corner of my eye, or on the street. Today was the closest he's come, and look at what happened."

She'd always been able to slip away, and yet it seemed like he'd known exactly where she would be today. Had Moose, or the man who'd introduced her to him, sold her out? No, Moose had come out and confronted the man with a shotgun. The man who made the introductions had been killed in a drive-by the week before.

Zoe rubbed her hands down her face. That random "accident" suddenly didn't seem so random. Had this whole thing been a setup?

Jude didn't let up. "He didn't hurt you. Does he have other plans for you?"

She lifted her gaze to his. "I don't know."

That was the truth—ish. Zoe did know *why* the man wanted her, she didn't know what he was going to *do* with her.

Jude sighed, then started up the car.

"Are you taking me to the police, or turning me into your people?" She'd come so close to actually getting herself and her son and sister out of this. Instead, this was the end of the line. Unless she could somehow convince Jude she hadn't done anything to warrant being turned in.

Could she talk about it? That night had been so harrowing she didn't even know if she could say it out loud.

"I'm not taking you in," he said in a tight voice. Trying to convince himself?

Zoe glanced out the window, relieved he wasn't pushing her. If she asked, would he drive her where she wanted to go? There was only one way to find out. "Take the next exit." Zoe needed to hold her son. "Please." Her voice sounded small even to her own ears.

He took the exit. He could drop her a few streets over from the house her sister had rented with cash, and he would never know where she was headed. So long as he didn't follow her. She'd have to be careful.

Jude said, "I really want to take you back

to the office. You have no idea how badly I want to do that."

Zoe nodded, whether he saw it or not. She knew he'd locked the rear doors of the SUV while she'd been laugh-crying. She hadn't been oblivious.

"Maybe you should." It was tempting. So tempting. "But you should know, the last time I talked to the police I was followed home that same day. I never heard from the officer again, and I didn't want to call him if he was the one who betrayed me. After that, I went to my local church. I guess I figured at least God would be on a minister's side." She shook her head. *What a mess.* "No one can help me, Jude."

"Maybe I can."

"I can't trust you with what I know. As much as I want to, I can't tell you what I saw—" She slapped a hand over her own mouth to stop the flow of words.

"Why get in my SUV if you don't want my help?"

"I don't even know what I want." Maybe that was a lie, maybe she wanted the connection of someone else in the world—apart from her son and her sister—knowing she was here and that she needed help. Just *knowing*.

Jude frowned, but headed in the direction

she indicated. Ten minutes later he pulled into the neighborhood behind the one where the house was located. She could cross the park behind this street and cut through to the street behind.

"What is…"

She glanced over and saw him peer through the passenger window to a cloud of smoke. Zoe cracked the door and a waft of burning wood hit her nostrils.

"Fire."

THREE

Zoe practically dived out of the car and set off running down the street. Jude got out and locked the car, then chased after her as she ran down an alley between two houses.

He pursued her toward the fire. Her house? Did she know if there were people inside?

At the end of the alley, he stumbled off the sidewalk onto grass. The fence gave way to an open space. Trees and a playground. Jude had spent many Friday nights hanging out at parks just like this as a rebellious teen, pushing back against his father, a pastor. He'd excelled at doing what everyone said was wrong and had the scars to prove it.

Zoe tore across the park like everything she loved, or cared about, was in danger. Was she married? She had no ring, but some people didn't wear one. She could have a husband or boyfriend at home, though in his opinion no man worth anything sent a woman into a dangerous situation alone. And that was exactly what she'd done. Zoe had walked into—and out of—that Laundromat by herself.

Jude didn't know whether to be impressed or exasperated by her.

He followed Zoe until the source of the smoke was in view, a tiny square house whose peeling paint was now melting from the siding. She raced down the sidewalk, and he knew what she was going to do. It would be so tempting to go inside and try to save whoever she had left behind. To play the part of hero, instead of waiting for the fire department. But it was too dangerous—the fire was too advanced.

He pumped his arms and legs and caught up to her just as she was about to cross the grass. Jude grabbed her. Before she could wriggle out of his grip, he wrapped his arms around her. "Don't. You can't go in."

Hot wind blew at them as the flames licked at the house. All around the outside it was on fire. "Let me go!" She kicked her legs, but Jude didn't release her.

"You can't save them."

"I have to. Tyler—" She grunted, and struggled against him.

The knowledge she had a man in her life

stung, even though there was nothing between them. "The fire department—"

"Let go of me." She kicked at his shins.

A neighbor ran over. "I hooked up my hose." He thumbed the end and the pouring water sprayed in an arc.

Jude wrestled with Zoe, but she kicked him again. Then elbowed his side. He sucked in a breath and released his grip only a fraction, but it was enough for her. Zoe broke free. "Aim for the front door," she ordered the neighbor. "I have to get Tyler out."

She raced for the wet, scorched door. Jude ran with her. Zoe reached for the handle with her bare hand.

He yelled, "No!"

She turned to him, her gaze as scorching as the fire. "I'm going in and you aren't going to stop me."

"That handle will burn the skin off your hand."

Before she could bluster, or do anything else crazy, he kicked the wood beside the handle. The door splintered, but the lock remained intact. What on earth?

He checked the lock without touching it. A black substance had been poured inside the mechanism where the key would be inserted. To keep whoever was inside from getting out?

Jude shuddered. Zoe stepped up beside him, and he said, "Be careful." If she was going to risk her life, then Jude would go with her and make sure she didn't get hurt simply because her instinct to protect this Tyler overrode her common sense.

He held her elbow as she clambered over the broken door. Inside was thick with smoke. Jude unbuttoned his shirt, thankful his father had instilled in him the need for an under-shirt, and ripped it in two. He handed half of his dress shirt to her.

"Tie this over your nose and mouth." He couldn't help adding, "This is reckless. You aren't a firefighter, are you?" He was pretty sure she wasn't. A firefighter would have known about the handle.

"I'm not a firefighter."

"Then we should go outside. This is crazy." They couldn't even see anything, and yet Zoe knew where she was going. "Is this your house?"

She shot him a look, then yelled, "Tyler!" A second later, she yelled, "Ember!"

Who was Ember? "Who are we looking for? They probably ran out back when the fire started."

"Tyler is my son." Zoe made her way down

a hall. "Ember is my sister, and she was watching him."

"Your son?" He looked around. The outside had been far more burned than the interior seemed to be. The fire still raged, and yet in here there were no visible flames. It was like someone had doused every wall and door of the exterior and set it ablaze. Inside was scorched and hot, but not burning. Had Zoe's family been trapped inside a house burning down from the outside?

He shivered. "How old is Tyler?"

"He's seven, but he's tall for his age so everyone thinks he's older." There was a note of pride along with the worry. "I hope they got out. I do." She coughed. "But we can't wait to check while they could be suffocating in here."

"Instead it's us who are suffocating. Firefighters have equipment for this." He choked out the words through his raspy throat, but she wouldn't be swayed. "Thirty seconds. If you don't find them, I'm getting us out of here whether you agree or not, Zoe." He paused. "Is that even your real name?"

"Of course it is." She pushed open a door with her foot. A master bedroom. "Tyler. Ember." Zoe moved to the closet. Door open, empty. He followed her to the en suite bathroom. The curtain had been pulled down and discarded and the shower was running.

A squeak came from Zoe, and she rushed over. Jude followed to see what had caught her eye, and saw as she did the two huddled in the bathtub. Both soaking wet, a young woman with dark hair was curled around a little boy. The woman had a nasty burn up the outside of her arm.

Zoe crouched. "Tyler." She touched the woman's cheek. "Em."

Jude reached down and pressed two fingers to the woman's neck. She couldn't be more than nineteen. This was Zoe's sister?

Zoe gasped, but he said, "She has a pulse."

The boy's eyes snapped open. "Mom—" The word dissolved into coughing and Zoe reached for him. The woman never stirred.

Zoe held her son to her. "Tyler."

"We couldn't get out, Mom. He trapped us inside."

Tyler wrapped his arms around her neck, and Jude found himself wanting to soak in the sight of the two of them so closely entwined. The way he'd done with his mom as a kid when he got hurt. But there was no time for that now. "We have to get out of here."

He picked up the woman and they trailed back outside, and he handed the woman off to two EMTs. A firefighter strode over. "Anyone else inside?"

He looked at Zoe, who shook her head. She still hadn't released her son.

"Why'd you go in there? You could've died, and we'd have been pulling out four instead of two."

Jude waved the man away from Zoe, then said, "Go see the EMTs, okay?"

She nodded. She didn't need the fire chief's ire, even if it had been a crazy idea to go inside. He flashed his badge at the man. "Jude Brauer, Secret Service." Like that justified his actions.

"It was a dumb move."

Jude didn't back down. "They were trapped in there, but now everyone's safe."

The firefighter muttered something and wandered off. Truth was, Jude didn't want to think about why he'd followed Zoe into the house. What mattered was that her son and sister were alive, and none of them were too badly hurt.

So why didn't he think this was even close to being over?

Zoe pulled Tyler to her in a hug and just let herself feel his skinny, little-boy body against hers. His arms around her back, he mumbled something against her jacket. She relaxed her arms and he leaned back to look up at her with his soot-covered face. "I'm fine, Mom. But Aunty Ember isn't."

Zoe nodded. "Let's go see."

He needed to get checked out, as well. They walked hand in hand to the ambulance Ember had been loaded into. She still hadn't woken up. "Is she going to be okay?"

The EMT had Tyler sit up inside the ambulance, which he thought was awesome judging by his grin, and put an oxygen mask on him. "Breathe deep, kiddo." Then he pointed at Ember, passed out on the bed with an oxygen mask already over her nose and mouth. "She's your babysitter?"

"My sister." Ember was her stepsister, but that qualification didn't matter to either of them. Neither did the nearly ten-year age difference between Zoe and Ember. They were still close, and her younger sister had risked her life for Tyler.

Was that how the killer had found the house? Zoe hardly spoke to anyone in her old life anymore. Still, it was possible the house had been discovered because of their connection.

The EMT said, "I'm going to need some information on your sister."

Zoe reminded herself this wasn't an interrogation and answered his questions. Personal information, medical history. Finally, Zoe had maxed out on her ability to be cordial. "Is she going to be okay?"

They wouldn't be asking all that stuff if Ember wasn't going to make it, would they? She didn't want Tyler to hear it if Ember was still in danger, but she couldn't wait any longer for an answer.

"We need to get her to the hospital before we'll know for sure. Are you coming?"

Zoe glanced back to where Jude stood, still talking to the firefighter. Should she go?

"You and your son need to be checked out, as well."

She nodded and tore her gaze from him. "I know."

Still, she saw realization dawn at the last second.

The EMT said, "He isn't coughing. I suppose if you keep a close eye on him tonight, his pediatrician can see him first thing. Doesn't have to be at the hospital."

A hospital could be the safest place for them at this point.

"That sound okay?"

Zoe nodded. She glanced at Jude again, and he saw it. Broke off his conversation to make his way over to her. "Everything okay?"

"They're taking Ember in." Would he send them with her, call someone to protect them? She wanted it to be Jude. But how could she ask that when they barely knew each other?

Tyler tore off the mask, his eyes pleading. "I wanna stay with you."

Zoe nodded. She felt the same way.

Her son looked up at Jude like he was one of those expert warriors from his library books. The ones who fought bad guys on a daily basis and won, unscathed. Every time.

The EMT shook Tyler's hand, which her son thought was hilarious. "Take it easy, kid." Then he looked at her. "If he so much as coughs twice…"

She nodded. "I'll watch him closely."

"You, too." He gave her a pointed look. "Your son will likely be fine, but I don't want you taking any chances. Smoke is nothing to mess with."

"Understood."

Tyler launched himself from the ambulance into her arms. She hugged him and then lowered him to the ground. The doors were shut, and the flashing lights receded. She turned to Jude, not really knowing what they were supposed to do now.

Tyler tugged on her hand. "Jude, this is Tyler. My son." She smiled down at him.

"Tyler, this is Jude." She leaned down slightly and whispered, "He's a Secret Service agent."

Tyler's eyes widened and he looked at Jude with something a lot like awe. "Sweet."

Jude chuckled, but Zoe just couldn't find the energy to do the same. She said, "What are we supposed to do now?"

His eyes widened at her question.

"I'm sorry. I don't even know why I asked you that." He didn't know them, and certainly didn't owe them anything. "You helped me get Tyler and Ember from the house and I never thanked you."

He shook his head. "Of course." And yet he hadn't even known she had a son when he ran into that burning house with her.

"Seriously, I can't thank you enough."

Why did she want to fall into his arms for a hug? Or maybe cry. Or both. But she couldn't, because Tyler was relying on her to be strong. No one except Ember had helped her with him since her husband signed away his rights and left with his girlfriend.

Men couldn't be trusted. She knew that. And yes, she meant *all* men. Zoe had never met one who kept his word and didn't eventually choose himself over the people he should have cared about. She knew the trust issue went deep, because she'd even had a hard time fully trusting God.

Now she had no idea what she was going to do. Where they would live, or how they would even have clothes for tomorrow. "My duffel bag." She glanced toward the park. "I left it in your car."

"All locked up." He patted his pocket. "After we make sure the police are good, we can walk over—"

"Why do we need to talk to the police?" There were a couple of their cars here, the officers checking out what was happening.

"Because the fire was deliberately set. They're going to open an investigation and they need our statements."

Zoe didn't know what she could tell them. She hadn't even been here at the time the fire was set. Meanwhile her son and sister had been *trapped* inside with nothing but the knowledge they were about to be burned alive.

Jude frowned. "We just need to make sure we're free to go."

"I'm free." She could just leave, couldn't she?

So why then did she feel trapped?

"Zoe—" He stepped closer to her.

Stars blinked in the edges of her vision.

"Mom?"

Tyler's voice sounded far away.

"Zoe." Jude's warm hands settled on her shoulders. "You need to take a breath."

"I don't want to talk to the police." The words came out broken. She couldn't catch her breath. It hadn't gone well the last time, and he knew that. "I'm free to leave whenever I want."

"The way you left the Laundromat? That's running, and it doesn't mean you're free—it means you're being chased." He leaned in close. "Breathe, Zoe."

She didn't want to be having this conversation in front of Tyler, but Jude wasn't giving her another option. "We'll be safe. We just need my duffel and then we'll be *gone*."

"Where? Where are you going to go?"

"Does it matter?"

Jude sighed. Zoe moved to go around him, to get out of there. He sidestepped.

She frowned at him. "Let us go."

"I'm not keeping you here, I just want to make sure you're safe."

Zoe nearly laughed then. "We will be. I'm going to make sure of it."

"How?" He crossed his arms.

"I don't need your help. I already thanked you for what you've done. Please come to the car with us and I'll get my stuff and you can forget all about us."

"Like that's going to happen." The words were muttered, but she heard them nonetheless.

"I'm serious, Jude. You don't have to worry about us."

"You can say it as much as you want, but so far tonight a man almost shot you. He did shoot two other people. And your house burned down."

Tyler gripped her hand harder, and she circled him with her arms again. To make her feel better, or him?

Did it matter? Comfort was comfort, and they were a team.

Jude ran his hands through his hair. He let his hands drop to his sides. "You aren't going to let me help you?"

"Why do you want to?"

"What?"

"Why do you want to take care of me?"

"Because—"

Across the street a man stood, glaring at them. The man from the Laundromat. Same lifeless eyes, same bulky jacket. Did he have the gun he'd used to kill Moose hidden in there?

Zoe gasped. "That's him. That's the—"

Jude was already running across the street, chasing down the man. What did he want with her? Whatever it was, Tyler would be caught in the crossfire. "Come on."

She didn't need that duffel. Zoe would find the money to get by somewhere else. She had no idea where but that wasn't the point. She couldn't stay here right now.

Anywhere else would be safer than this.

FOUR

Jude raced after the man. Anger coursed through him, a burst of energy to his fatigued muscles. The long day. The shooting. The fire. All of it he left behind with every step he took as he sprinted across the street like it was six in the morning on the trail and he was freshly rested from a full night of sleep. *Thank You, Lord.*

He'd seen the moment recognition sparked in the man's eyes—the only sign of life he'd noticed since that poor attempt at humor in the Laundromat. This man wasn't going to hurt anyone else. Not if Jude could do something about it.

One of the cops yelled, but Jude couldn't explain. He just called after the man, "Secret Service. Stop!"

He didn't. This guy clearly cared more about the freedom to do whatever he wanted than the law. And the fact that he'd placed himself firmly on the wrong side of it.

Seconds later, Jude got within touching distance. He grabbed the man's arm and got a handful of jacket before his fingers lost grip. More speed. The corner at the end of the street was coming up. Jude could cut it slightly, and try to tackle the man. He kept pumping his arms and legs as best he could in the suit.

The man pivoted at the corner and before Jude could figure out the move, his elbow came up. Pain burst through Jude's skull and light flashed behind his eyes, but he didn't go down. He grasped on to the jacket again, but the man shrugged out of it and raced away, leaving Jude with his jacket and nothing else. Jude took off after him, but only got two steps before he weaved with dizziness and collided with a fence. Splinters raked his arm and he hissed.

The cops ran up. One said, "What—"

There wasn't time to let him finish; the gunman was getting away. "Murder suspect." Jude sucked in a breath and hung his head. It hurt. He'd probably have a headache for days. He reached up and gently felt his forehead. There was a knot already.

One cop took off after the suspect. The other stood with Jude. "You all right?"

He felt around the jacket. It smelled like gasoline. Had he set the fire, or simply been close enough to it that the scent of accelerant was on his clothes? There was nothing in the bottom pockets, but the inside pocket held something bulky. He found a wallet and opened it. Two hundred in cash was folded up along with a pharmacy receipt for Oxycodone and a driver's license.

"Want me to take that?"

Jude took a photo of both sides of the license so he could look it up later, then handed it over to the cop, who could add it to evidence. "It's probably a fake so he can get his meds." He gave the officer the name of the detectives investigating the Laundromat shooting.

The officer nodded. "I'll get this squared away for ya."

Jude pushed off the wall and headed back to the now smoldering house. Only the smell of the fire remained. Even Zoe and Tyler were gone. He searched up and down the street for them. She'd done it again, ditched him even though her duffel was locked in his Suburban.

He knew she didn't trust him. That went both ways. But why did it bother him so much? It wasn't like they knew each other.

Part of him wanted to stick with her—to convince her that she should trust him with what was happening to her. Sure, if he got answers that helped him with his case at the same time, then great. Moose was dead, but Zoe might know something about the man's business.

In return, he could help her be safe, even find whoever was targeting her. So long as he didn't have to chase anybody else. The way he was feeling right now, they would probably get away, as the gunman had.

Jude blew out a breath. Why was he messing this up at every turn? He was supposed to be on the right path now, doing the right thing. Career first, and then personal life. Yet it still seemed as though he couldn't get his life right. No wonder she didn't trust him. She was probably right to simply rely on herself and not invite him to assist.

But whether she was willing to ask for his help or not, it was obvious that she needed it. The fact that Tyler was in the picture wasn't a negative, but it had to be taken into account. They were both clearly in danger.

Zoe and her family had been targeted separately.

Jude sighed again, and started toward the park. Maybe they'd headed to the SUV as a safe haven and were waiting for him there. Twice tonight the same guy had shown up.

Why did he want Zoe, but not seem to want her dead? The fire might have been a statement, but had the killer gone out of his way to do that so Zoe would find it? That seemed overly elaborate.

It made more sense that they were all in danger. With her son's life being used to threaten Zoe.

Jude couldn't ask her what the man wanted with her because she wasn't around that he could see. He clicked the locks and opened the back door. The black duffel lay on the seat, and he pulled the zipper back. His eyes widened. Inside were rolls of twenties, secured by rubber bands. Tens of thousands of dollars by the look of it. He whistled.

"You need to give that to me."

He spun around, half expecting her to be holding a weapon on him, given her threatening tone of voice. There was no gun in her hand, but the determination in her expression made it clear she wouldn't be backing down.

"Maybe you don't need my help after all," he said. "Looks like you have the means to go anywhere you want. Is that what you were looking for in Moose's office, new ID's? Passports, maybe?"

Her eyes flared. Bingo.

"You could flee the country. Except they'll

likely come after you still. Which means you and Tyler will live the rest of your lives with targets on your backs, never knowing which day will be the one they'll find you."

She paled, but didn't say anything. Tyler looked more mad than scared.

"Purchasing fake identification is a crime."

Zoe lifted her chin at that. "I didn't purchase anything. Not yet anyway."

He was almost proud of her for the way she stood her ground. The woman had backbone—she had to or she'd have crumbled long before now. She likely would have purchased the ID had Moose not been killed. What had pushed her to such lengths? Her house had burned down after that decision had been made. After the man left her alive.

Jude was fine being the one responsible for the fact that she was alive, unharmed and with her son. If Jude was going to help then he needed to know why she was being threatened.

He just couldn't help the errant thought that the attempt to buy fake ID's wasn't her only foray into the wrong side of the law. Dangerous men were after her—and her unwillingness to trust the authorities sent up red flags.

"Did you…do something?" He didn't want to talk plainly in front of Tyler, not knowing what the boy was aware of and what he wasn't.

"Is that why you won't talk to the police?" Perhaps he should simply load them both into the SUV and drive them to his office to explain it all.

"You think I did something?" She looked almost as though he'd betrayed her, which helped reassure him. "I know it looks bad, but I'm not the criminal here."

The boy spoke then. "My mom hasn't done anything wrong!"

"Tyler." She admonished him with just his name.

Jude held up one hand. "I'm a cop, Tyler. I have to ask *every* question, even the hard ones."

Zoe turned to Tyler. "Why don't you sit in the car?" She didn't give him an option; she simply steered him to the open door. "Don't worry about Jude, okay? I can handle him." Tyler climbed over the duffel and lay down, and Zoe shut the door.

What could she say to Jude to explain this whole mess? She was so tired and frazzled from the whole exhausting day she didn't even know where to begin.

She shook her head and realized her hair was still pinned from being under the wig. She reached up and started to pull out the clips.

He stared at her.

"What?" Maybe she was more tired than she'd thought because Jude Brauer was watching her as if he might be interested. That didn't make sense, did it? He thought she was *a criminal*. And even if she could understand why he might think that way, the accusation still hurt. She hadn't done anything but try to be a good mother and provide for her son.

"You look…" His voice trailed off.

"Like I was in a fire?" She cocked her head to the side, pulling out the last pin and letting her chin-length brown hair hang loose.

"You know what I mean."

Yes, she did. Unfortunately. She was totally wrong about his interest, of course—the man thought she looked like a bedraggled waif. Lovely. "You could take us to a motel, I guess. Unless you have a better idea."

He studied her, then said, "I might."

Zoe lifted her arms, then let them fall back to her sides. "I'm open to suggestions. But only because it's been a long day and I'm exhausted, my son is exhausted and he's been through a traumatic experience."

Zoe wiped a stray tear from her cheek and shut her eyes. "I have no idea where we're going to go now, or what we're going to do." When she opened them his face was soft, his eyes warm. Compassion had been in short supply lately. She didn't want to soak it up now, especially from a man she wasn't sure she could trust, but it was like an unexpected present.

"I can help you, Zoe." His voice was soft. "I want to help you and Tyler be safe."

"But only if I tell you everything?"

"I know you don't trust me, but you can trust the cops."

"The first one I talked to was killed the same day. I told you. And I doubt it was simply a coincidence, given there have been a whole lot of seemingly unrelated coincidences happening to me lately."

"Because of something you saw?"

She'd let that slip before, and apparently he hadn't forgotten it. Zoe nodded. "Yes."

"So you're a witness."

"And Tyler and I are in danger because of it." She clutched two handfuls of her hair and tugged, but it didn't relieve her frustration. "I tried to do the right thing, Jude. I really did. But I feel like the world is against me, and I can't get out in front of it long enough for something to go right." She took a breath. "Now Ember is in the hospital, and I don't even know if she's going to make it. But I'm too scared I'll put her in danger if I go and see her."

He stepped closer. "I can't promise you everything will be okay. I don't have the kind of power to guarantee that. I will pray, and I'm not going to stop praying for you until all this has been resolved. Until you and Tyler have nothing to worry about except him getting to soccer practice on time."

"He plays football."

Jude said, "You know what I mean."

"I do. And thank you. You've done so much, I feel guilty asking you for more."

"Don't." He shook his head. "It's my pleasure to help you."

She thought for a second he might hug her, but instead he stepped back and motioned to the car.

"Get in. I'll find you somewhere safe you can clean up and get some rest. In the morning we can make a plan to get you and Tyler safe permanently."

She climbed in the back, tired enough to just hand him her whole life and ask him to fix it. But she had to hold back. No man had ever proved to her that was a good move. Every time she thought she'd found the exception, she'd just get her heart broken again.

Zoe only knew one way to trust and that

was all in, no holds barred. It had gotten her in trouble in nearly every relationship. Now she saw the same traits in Tyler. Ever since Nathan had left, she'd been so careful in the influences she allowed around her son, not wanting him to get attached to anyone who might hurt him. If they let Jude into their lives it would end badly for both of them.

Sure, Jude would probably fix her problems regardless. She could see he was capable, even though he hadn't said whether he'd caught that man or not. She figured it meant he hadn't. But even with the gunman still on the loose, Jude wasn't any less of a hero to her. He'd stuck by her side.

She just wished she could believe it would continue. That he'd never leave, or fail her. But that was human nature. It was better to simply rely on herself. She understood her own weaknesses. Jude could help, but she wouldn't give him control of her life. And she wasn't going to count on him—not completely.

He had a job to do after all, as well as a personal life of his own. One he wouldn't want clogged up by her and her son. Men didn't like that; they liked their space. "Aren't you going to fix Mrs. McAffrey's sink tomorrow?"

He pulled up at a red light and glanced back

to flash her a grin in the dark of the car. "I guess I did say I was going to do that."

She nodded, though she wasn't sure he could see her. Zoe adjusted her hold on her son, trying not to let the middle seat belt dig into his tummy too much. "I'm sure Tyler and I will be okay." They'd need clothes, a backpack. Her son would need books or games to occupy him when he got restless. The list of things flitted through her mind, overwhelming her.

Zoe glanced at the roadside speeding past and tried to pray, as Jude had suggested he would. It seemed so false. How had God helped her so far? She was too tired to figure out the answer.

Half an hour later Jude pulled into the parking lot of a church.

"Uh…" Had God been listening? Maybe He thought she needed to really seek Him, so He'd directed Jude to bring her to a church. *Busted.* Okay, so they hadn't exactly been on the same page lately, but really? "Is there something you're trying to tell me?"

Jude put the car in park and turned to her. "What's that?"

"Nothing." She shook her head, not ready to share this, either. Jude didn't need to know that she and God weren't exactly on speaking terms. It was enough of a struggle to convince herself to tell him exactly what was going on, let alone adding her spiritual problems.

"Want me to get Tyler?"

He wanted to carry her son? "Sure. Thanks." Why was it so easy to say that? She was exhausted enough she could accept the help, but didn't think it was the real reason she was so comfortable with him.

He strode around to a side door of the church like he was arriving home after a long day of work. At the door, he handed her his keys. "The gold one."

Zoe let them in, and Jude flicked the light on to reveal a long hall. "There are some rooms back here—one has a set of bunk beds you guys can use, bathroom is attached. The room is between two exits." He motioned up and down the hall. "In case something happens, you can get out easily."

Zoe nodded. "I really appreciate—" she hardly knew where to start "—all of this." The duffel was heavy on her shoulder, and the quicker they got to sleep the quicker they could get up and get out of here. Jude wouldn't need to worry then.

A man cleared his throat. But not Jude. Zoe spun around to find an older man in pajamas and slippers. His bald head reflected the overhead light. He almost looked like—

The old man shifted. "I guess you have some things to explain, considering y'all smell like smoke and look like you're still in shock." He paused. "Not exactly the normal scenario for when your son brings a woman and child home to meet you."

FIVE

The next morning Jude sat at the kitchen table the way he had every morning his entire childhood. The only thing that had changed was the oven—the old one had finally died a few years ago. The new one looked as out of place there as Jude felt. Dressed in the gym clothes he kept in the SUV's trunk, he took a sip of the strong coffee his father had made. The man got up earlier than anyone he'd ever met—a throwback to the old days as a marine. Jude didn't mind early mornings, but he needed time to wake up.

His mom walked by and squeezed his shoulder, then leaned down and kissed the top of his head like he was still six.

"Mornin'."

She chuckled. "Good morning, darling."

Leanne Brauer was a stocky woman who'd given him her height and her blond hair, though his was darker. In comparison, his father had brown hair and was slender except for his round middle. His mom bustled about the kitchen, getting out flour and sugar. Pancakes? Jude sat a little straighter in his chair.

"I checked on Zoe and Tyler. They're still resting." She got the blueberries out of the fridge.

He grinned to himself and took another sip. "Jude?"

He glanced up at her. "Yeah, Mom?"

"Did you hear me?"

He said, "Zoe and Tyler are good."

She studied him a second longer than was probably necessary. That "Mom Look" they used to see everything, know everything. He'd never been able to keep secrets from her.

Thankfully, his dad entered right then, so he didn't have to explain everything to her, the way he would have in another moment if left alone with her Look. He didn't want to tell the story twice anyway, and he'd made excuses last night. They'd been able to clean up and go to bed instead of having a long conversation. From Zoe's flush of gratitude he'd figured it was the right call—even if she also seemed like she had more to say to his dad.

"Haven't seen you in a few Sundays." Andrew Brauer clapped him on the shoulder.

Jude knew what that meant. "Darren is

doing a great job taking care of the teens, right? He doesn't need my help." In fact, since Darren's arrival as the new youth pastor Jude had been floundering, trying to figure out where he fit in his dad's ministry.

His dad poured a cup of coffee, kissed his wife on the cheek and sat across from Jude at the battered table where they'd shared countless meals through the years. "So work has been busy?"

Jude nodded, unsure if he should feel guilty or not that cases often caught a new lead on the weekend, sometimes interfering with church attendance. There was nothing he could do about that. Working as a federal agent wasn't like a lot of other Monday-to-Friday, nine-to-fives. Jude called often enough, and they had dinner every few weeks.

"Huh." His dad took another sip.

Jude did the same. He wasn't straying in his faith; he just found it hard to get to church sometimes. And he honestly didn't know if the ministry his father had him in was what he actually wanted to do. Youth ministry brought him into contact with kids he wouldn't normally have been able to reach otherwise, and he enjoyed spending time with them. But he was still mostly all about work. Because work *had* to come first, and sometimes that meant his attention to the ministry suffered.

"I'll try to be there this Sunday, okay?"

His dad nodded but said nothing, which was fine with Jude. When his mom glanced back at him he understood enough. They weren't happy with all of his choices, but they got it.

And why wasn't that okay for him? Jude only wanted them to be proud, but they really wouldn't be unless he was with them in the ministry 24/7, right? That was the only thing he could figure would make them completely happy. If he "ploughed the field" alongside them, as his father put it.

Jude would rather find his own field instead of them always pushing him to do more, to be more. To give more of his time to what they thought was best for him. In the end he'd wound up pushing himself at work *and* in ministry. Deferring what he wanted until he was "ready" instead of having what he wanted right now. Until he was satisfied he was doing the right thing, he was pushing off the life— the family—he actually wanted. He'd pulled away in ministry, but the family thing was a whole different ball game.

Tyler wandered into the room. Jude pushed out a chair with his foot and the kid sat beside him. "Doing okay?"

Tyler nodded. Jude's mom put a glass of milk in front of him and he sucked it down. His mom chuckled. "Seems familiar."

Jude shared a smile with her and then looked Tyler over. Physically he seemed fine, but who knew about his mental state? "I called the hospital. Your aunt Ember is still sleeping. They're going to let me know when she wakes up. They also said it isn't necessarily bad that she hasn't woken up."

Tyler said, "'Kay." Then asked, "Did you catch that man last night?"

"No, buddy. I'm sorry." The detective had left a voice mail on Jude's phone with the news.

"I don't want him coming here." Tyler shivered.

Jude shifted his chair closer, just a fraction. "That's why I brought you here. To be safe." He motioned to his dad. "This is Mr. Andrew, and that's Mrs. Leanne. They're my mom and dad, and they're going to help me keep you and your mom safe."

Tyler didn't look all the way convinced, but Jude didn't know what else to say.

His mom took two steps over from the griddle she had heating up on the counter. "Do you like blueberry pancakes, Tyler?"

The boy nodded to her and then glanced

back at Jude. "Someone set fire to the house, and we couldn't get out. They locked the doors, and we couldn't get them open."

His mom stiffened, but didn't make a noise. His dad stared. Jude ignored them both and held Tyler's attention. He'd been right. They'd been deliberately trapped.

"The police are going to find him, and I'm going to help you and your mom be safe." He figured there wasn't much that would convince the kid after last night, but he wanted Tyler to know he was on the job.

The boy fingered his glass.

"You should show him your tree house."

Jude started at his mom's suggestion. "The tree house?"

"I'm sure Tyler would love to see your tree house."

The boy had perked up. Jude nearly smiled. "What do you say—after breakfast do you want to go check out the tree house?"

Tyler nodded.

"It might need some repairs, but I'm sure we can manage something."

Jude had to go to work at some point, but he'd already checked in this morning. Spending time with Zoe and Tyler would help him with his case if he could learn more about Moose and his operation. If it was time spent that was also enjoyable, and kept them safe, what did it matter? It wasn't as if he was neglecting his work.

Zoe's face filled his mind, her wide eyes both filled with fear and gratitude. She was beautiful, but his reaction to her could simply be because she was here and she needed his help. That wasn't a good basis for anything serious, or he'd have settled for "Ms. Right Now" a long time ago. The fact that Zoe was a possible witness in his case as well just made the whole thing a lot stickier.

Jude didn't want to get his heart broken, or break the heart of a woman who only felt close to him because she needed his help. He should keep things professional, and forget about the fact that he was attracted to Zoe. While he figured he could trust her, the reality was that he didn't know much about who she was. Or what she had done.

And none of his reasons for postponing a relationship until later had changed.

She appeared then, freshly showered with her wet hair hanging straight around her face. It was adorable, and tested his resolve to keep things businesslike between them.

"Good—" He cleared his throat. "Good morning, Zoe."

Jude didn't miss the look his mom gave him.

* * *

An hour later they walked across the grassy area behind the church. Zoe set her hand on her very full—but still flat—stomach. She was as devout about doing crunches as she was about drinking coffee. "That was a lot of pancakes."

Jude grinned. "Feeling like you got shot with a bear tranquilizer is the best part of a carb-loaded breakfast."

She had to laugh. He was kind of charming in the morning light, and he'd kept her son entertained all through breakfast with stories of his childhood antics. Getting lost in the attic of the church, toilet papering the elders' cars with his sister and playing pranks on his youth leader at camp.

His parents had added details, and though they'd seemed mortified by their son's antics, they smiled as they spoke of them. It was clear they loved Jude very much. Just as they loved his elder sister, who Jude explained was "the good one." Zoe had learned that she was married to the associate pastor of a church in Idaho, and had three kids.

"Why do you look sad?"

She stopped beside him, unsure how much to explain.

Tyler said, "I see it!"

"Okay, go for it." She walked over to her son and fluffed his hair. "Just be careful."

Jude said, "Watch for wobbly boards and try to steer clear of them, okay?"

Tyler yelled, "Okay!" as he ran to the big oak with a monster tree house perched up high. A little boy's dream.

She watched him for a minute, until Jude touched her elbow. "You were saying?"

"I'm pretty sure I wasn't," she said. "But since you asked so nicely…" She couldn't help the wry smile.

Jude even returned it. "You don't have to tell me. I was just curious."

She knew he wanted her to trust him. The only problem was life had taught her that people weren't trustworthy. "I looked sad because you have a lovely family. And it sounds like you had a very loving childhood."

"And that's a bad thing?"

Zoe glanced at her son, and not just to check on him. She waited until she saw his head peek out the tree house window. Certain he was out of hearing range, she said, "Mine makes me sad. In comparison." Why get into the gory details of shouting matches, all those slamming doors and recriminations?

His gaze softened. "I'm sorry."

She shook her head. "It's done now. Over.

My stepdad is who-knows-where, and my mom…" Zoe swallowed. "She passed away before Tyler was born. Only days before, to be precise. Ember came to live with us, and I practically raised her."

They'd shared so much joy over his impending birth, and even with their strained history she and her mom had been trying to salvage a relationship. Tyler would have brought them closer together as mother and daughter. But that was never meant to be.

Ember had been the best part of her life before Tyler. Helping her mom by taking care of her little sister had prepared her more than anything for motherhood.

Jude touched her shoulder. Zoe rubbed her hands down her tired face, then said, "It was a long time ago."

"Can I ask about… Tyler's father?"

"Nathan and I were married for four years." They'd only gotten married when she found out she was pregnant, a move she wasn't entirely proud of. Like a lot of things in her life. "He took off just after Tyler's third birthday, and he got remarried—to his secretary—as soon as the ink on our divorce papers was dry."

Jude blew out a breath. "I'm sorry."

"I'm not the innocent party, but thank you.

He didn't do right by us, but neither was I the perfect wife. And I'm certainly not the perfect mom. There are a lot of things in my life I'd like to have done differently, but I can't go back and change them. I can only try to make better choices from now on."

"That's admirable."

Zoe shrugged. "I figure mostly it's just trying not to mess up Tyler's life. He should have a better start than I did, and all this danger—gunmen and houses burning down—isn't helping. Now he's scared for Ember, as well. She's all the extended family he has."

Jude pulled out his phone. Which was kind of rude. Then he showed her a photo on the screen.

She shook her head. "You got his driver's license?"

"When I chased him last night I got his jacket, and the wallet was inside. The police have it."

She peered closer at the picture, then shuddered. "That is him. *Tucker Wilson*. Is that his name?"

"I'm going to run it through the system when I go to work. I'm pretty sure it's fake, maybe even one of Moose's, but this should give me enough to start figuring out who he is and why he's targeting you."

She nodded. What would Jude say when he found out she'd seen a dead woman, and then just run away? She'd tried to call the cops.

"If Moose did make the drivers' license, then maybe he sold me out to Tucker Wilson for some reason."

Jude just waited.

"I want to trust you, Jude. You haven't given me any reason not to."

"Maybe we can meet up with the police today. The ones investigating Moose's murder. You're an eyewitness, and it would save them time having to figure out what happened if you can explain it to them."

Did he think her last statement meant she was prepared to tell everything now?

She didn't like the idea of wasting the cops' time when she could give them the answers they were looking for. The idea of trusting them not to dismiss her statement wouldn't dissipate. Or the fact that they could get hurt.

She said, "I've been trying to do the right thing since Nathan left. Getting a job. Ember helped out watching Tyler after school when her dad let her—she's a freshman in college now. We moved into an apartment, and I was paying bills. Catching up on the taxes Nathan never paid for us while we were married." Zoe bit her lip as tears stung her eyes.

"Now this? All because I stayed late at work for the overtime."

"What happened, Zoe? What happened that it has a murderer and arsonist after you?"

"I was headed for my car. The lot under the office where I worked is underground. It was mostly empty that late at night. I heard something behind me. Arguing. The man hit the woman, and she fell. I don't know if she hit her head, or something else but…she didn't get back up."

Zoe shut her eyes at the memory of the man, standing over the woman. She'd been so still. "He saw me there, and I tried to call for help, but there's no signal down there. I ran, and when I looked back he was loading her into the backseat. He glared at me like I was next."

She shuddered. "I called the police after I pulled onto the street and told them what I saw. I gave them all my contact information, but no one ever followed up with me. I called the police station the next day and no one knew what I was talking about. The man asked me if I was drunk and then hung up on me. What cop does that?"

Jude frowned. "It does seem strange."

"A week later I made contact with a detective because I was being followed. Harassed. You know what happened then." She bit her lip, remembering back to the parking lot. "I saw blood under her head. Even if the body had been moved before the police arrived, there has to have been something there, some evidence for the police to find. So why didn't they investigate?"

"The man," Jude said. "Who was he?"

She waited, then said, "My boss."

"Zoe—"

"Mom!" Tyler ran back to her. "Mom, that tree house is *epic*."

She smiled and hugged her son to her. "Awesome." She shouldn't be grateful for the interruption, but Jude had most likely been about to ask her exactly who her boss was. She wasn't ready to share that. Jude would most likely be familiar with a man as powerful as the one she had worked for. The company was well-known in Salt Lake.

"I'm gonna go back up there!"

"Okay." She gave her son a squeeze, and he ran off again.

"You can trust me, Zoe."

She didn't look at him. She couldn't, or he would know how scared she was. "My boss sent Tucker Wilson to look for me. He could show up at any moment. I won't see him coming. How am I supposed to protect Tyler from that kind of threat?"

"You let me help you. I'm going into work, and I'll find out who Tucker Wilson really is. The police are running down the leads, as well. We'll put him away. All you have to do is stay here where it's safe."

She nodded.

"And tell me who your boss is."

Zoe swallowed. Wind whipped through the trees. Jude glanced around. "You should probably get Tyler inside, just to be safe."

She called her son over.

"I have to debrief with the task force for the case I'm working on, but by the time it's done I'll hopefully know who our guy is. Okay?"

She couldn't nod, or answer. The police could find Tucker, but how would it stop her boss from sending someone else? Someone who would pull the trigger.

Tyler reached them, and glanced between her and Jude. "What, Mom?"

"Let's go inside now." She didn't wait, just led her son back to the church building and the attached home Jude's parents lived in. Jude, who wanted to help figure this out for her. Who wanted her to trust him.

She really needed to tell him.

Jude held the door, and Tyler trailed inside.

Zoe stopped beside him. "I worked for BioWell Pharmaceuticals."

Jude gaped. "You saw Alan Reskin murder someone?"

SIX

Jude spent the drive to work going over and over it. She'd been employed by the same company he was investigating. In what department? She could know more than he'd realized. She could know everything he needed to crack this case wide-open. He'd wanted to haul her to the office, but the concern on Tyler's face had stalled him.

She'd seen her boss, Alan Reskin, one of the most powerful men in Salt Lake City, murder a woman. Another man had been sent by Reskin to hurt her family. It was enough to make him want to give her no choice but to accept protective custody.

Jude had to get permission first, though. He pulled into his favorite parking space behind the building and headed up the elevator. He swiped his key card and checked in.

Once he reached his desk, the first thing he did was get on his computer, upload the photo of the driver's license from his phone and start the search. A couple of people said, "Hi," and he returned the greeting. The other agents he worked with were great, though he wouldn't call them close friends. Jude enjoyed working alone too much for that.

He grabbed a coffee and the task force morning meeting started. They weren't happy when he explained what had happened to Moose. His boss shot him a look Jude didn't like. Then he told them about BioWell.

The room erupted.

Agent Milsner, one of Jude's colleagues, said, "You think she's involved in the money laundering?"

Jude didn't like the agent's tone at all. He waited until the ruckus calmed down, then said, "With criminals? No way."

She wasn't lying about having seen a murder, either. Despite what a couple of the agents thought. He'd been trained to spot the indicators that someone might be lying, and she'd shown none of them. If it was an act then she deserved an award because he'd never met a person that good at acting. She was scared, and he'd seen the threat for himself. The danger in her life was obvious but he didn't believe the man after her was acting alone. He couldn't have shot up the Laundromat and then gone immediately to burn down her house. There hadn't been time to line things up that perfectly.

So was there more than one threat, or was she being targeted by multiple people? There could be a head on this snake, calling the shots over the money and Zoe. Her boss? Alan Reskin seemed professional enough, but anyone could be pushed to kill under the right circumstances. Jude didn't like not knowing all the answers.

No one looked particularly convinced of Zoe's innocence, so he said, "If she knows anything I'll find out. But I want her and her son protected."

Milsner lifted his chin, gung-ho as usual. "I say we get a warrant. Raid the company and dig through what we find."

"We'll wait for something more solid. The DA will never go for it based on what we have so far." Agent Daniels, his boss, sat at the far end of the conference room table. He glanced at Jude. "I'll assign agents to keep an eye on Reskin, but I want to know what Zoe knows. You have one day to find out."

It wasn't protective custody, where Zoe and Tyler would be secure in a house the Secret Service had complete control over, and it wasn't nothing, either. But one day? "Sir—"

"You're all dismissed."

Jude made a move to leave with the other agents but his boss waylaid him with a flick of his hand. Jude sat and the room emptied. At the last moment Milsner glanced back with a smirk, even though this was nothing like getting called to the principal's office.

"You think you can get her talking?"

Jude thought on it. "I think there's a good chance. I'm going to work on that as well as other leads." The purple-haired woman was a bust. She'd checked out of the hospital and refused to give the police anything.

Daniels nodded. "This woman knows about Moose's operation, which helps the cops unpack possible motives for his murder. But how is she an asset to our case?"

Daniels leaned against the table because his new left knee was titanium and bothered him until he took the weight off it. He wore wide-rimmed glasses and had a military haircut. He wasn't what most people probably pictured when they thought of Secret Service agents. He looked like what he was—a sharp and capable man who was very good at his job.

Jude respected him, and not just because he pushed Jude for every single result he got. He wanted Jude to know precisely why he was doing this by asking him to reiterate it now.

"Aside from the murder she saw three weeks ago, Zoe can also potentially supply me with information on the kind of transactions Moose was making. The killer from the Laundromat—who she can identify—."

"As can you now, right?"

Jude nodded. He had seen Tucker himself, right after Moose had been shot, chased the man after the fire and gotten his wallet. "The killer has his own identity, which I believe Moose fabricated for him. Zoe is in the middle of this. The fact that she might have witnessed a murder committed by her boss could be part of it. Our investigation into the pharmaceutical company might have nothing to do with Zoe, depending on what her job was, but I'll find out either way."

"You think she saw an unsolved murder?"

"Possibly, though she said the cops made no record of it. There might be an open case on some detective's desk, but there also might not." Jude needed her to talk, otherwise he'd have to do the legwork. It could take him weeks to figure out what she'd seen and who was involved.

"You may need to hand this off to PD if the threads of your case tie off and their hunt for this Tucker Wilson is still ongoing." Agent Daniels lifted off the table.

"Yes, sir."

"Run it down, Agent Brauer." He tapped the tabletop with his knuckles and left the room.

Jude mostly figured that meant "Good job," or, "Go get 'em, son." But he didn't know for sure. His boss was solid. Jude would miss working under him when one—or both—of them moved up in the ranks of the Secret Service. It was another part of why he'd put off having a serious relationship with any woman.

Jude didn't know what city he'd be working in ten years from now—or what he would be doing. The divorce rate among agents was high, and many of them retired before starting families. Still, there were happily married agents in the Secret Service. One was a director on the president's detail Jude had met a few years ago.

He mulled it over as he went back to his desk and logged on to his computer. The first time he'd left it unlocked and walked away the other agents had changed his desktop background to an extremely embarrassing picture of Jude and a bunch of cats. It had been the worst graphic he'd ever seen, several pictures badly overlaid, but the point had been made: don't leave your info for anyone to get into. The stuff agents looked at was no one else's business, and bad security habits led to slacking, which led to leaking confidential information, even if he didn't mean to do so. Security was paramount.

Once he logged in, Jude got to work breaking down the history on the driver's license. The identity was a strong fabrication. The last known address was probably fake, but the electronic record was far more convincing than a person who'd simply begun to exist on the date the license was issued.

Moose was good, but Jude had access to multiple agency and government databases. He ran the picture through all of them and added a prayer he would get some information back soon. It wouldn't necessarily get him an identity on the man, but everything had to be followed up just in case it got him an answer. Often the answer would be to a question he hadn't even asked.

Jude sent a couple of emails to the detectives, and cleared out his inbox while he waited for a reply to his offer of a meeting between Zoe and the detectives investigating the Laundromat homicide. She had shared about BioWell, and she hadn't precisely said she wouldn't talk to the cops. He was pushing her offer of trust, and prayed it wouldn't backfire on him.

He'd have to go through Moose's office and try to find a paperwork trail that would help the task force investigation. See if he couldn't discover who was behind it that way. Moose was dead, his entire business now part of a police investigation. Jude needed the cooperation of the detectives to get access. Hopefully they'd share what they found.

Five minutes later he got an email. The detectives from the Laundromat wanted to meet with Zoe.

"Right now?" Zoe gripped the phone Jude's father had handed her. Andrew stood close by, a worried look on his face. She tried to send the older man a calm smile, but didn't think he believed it.

On the other end of the phone Jude said, "I'm driving back to the church now. They agreed to meet us at a diner downtown. A neutral location, so you can give them a statement while we eat. The whole thing will take less than an hour."

He was trying to reassure her it wasn't a big deal, but tell that to her stomach. Just the idea of eating while she talked about blood and death made those pancakes want to resurface. She swallowed hard and tried to think of happy things.

He hung up before she could finish processing the idea, and then she had to tell Tyler she was going out. He'd given up on the book Leanne had found him, and opted instead to stare at the window as though threats lurked there. She didn't want him to be scared, but she wouldn't lie and tell him there was nothing to worry about. They weren't safe.

"You're leaving?"

She nodded. "I don't want to, but I have to talk to the police."

He got up. "I want to come with you."

What mom was able to resist that? "I think you should stay here, Ty. Andrew and Leanne will keep you company until I get back."

He hugged her, his movements frantic. Zoe rubbed the back of his head, realizing he needed a haircut. "I'll be back before you know it." She didn't want him listening to what she had to say to the police. He was already scared enough, though he didn't know the details. He simply read her emotions and reflected them back without realizing.

"I know you're scared. So am I." She tugged on him until he leaned back and looked at her. Then she said, "I'll be careful, and Jude will be with me. You'll be here with Andrew and Leanne, and I'll be back. Soon."

"I want to go and see Aunty Ember. She's in the hospital all alone."

"It's okay to be alone when you're sleeping,

you know that. The doctor said she might not wake up for hours." They'd told her as much when she'd called, though it was debatable whether this much time unconscious was a good thing or not.

Still, if it made him happier, she would figure out a way to get him to the hospital to see her sister. "I'll talk to Jude, and when I get back we'll go. Maybe she'll be awake by then."

"I want to see her today, Mom."

She narrowed her eyes and tried to inject some humor into this completely unfunny situation. "Are you bossing me?"

He grinned. "I'm getting bigger."

"You could be ten feet tall, and I'd still be in charge."

"We'd be equals, though. Your votes can't outvote mine if I'm taller."

She narrowed her eyes at him. Everyone knew parents' votes counted for two and kids' only one; that way a consensus could be reached more easily. "Maybe. I'll take it to committee."

"They'll say I'm right." Even though there was no committee, and he probably didn't even know what that meant.

Zoe kissed his head and snuggled with him until Jude got there.

Being with the Secret Service agent in the

car was nowhere near as comforting as time with her son. Especially since Jude barely said anything to her the entire way downtown while Zoe stared out the window.

Was this really what her life had become? She'd been trying her best to be a good mom and provide for her son by getting a good job doing admin in the accounts department. The best position she'd been able to find with no degree and only minimal qualifications.

Then one night everything had changed. She shuddered at the memory of that woman lying on the dirty concrete. The man standing over her. Their exchanged words had been vicious, and she'd fought back. But he'd bested her with one swing and she'd fallen.

Jude adjusted the vents and the temperature dial. "Are you cold?"

Zoe swallowed past the lump in her throat. "I'm ready to be done with this and get back to Tyler."

"He's safe, you know."

"I thought he was safe with Ember, but I was wrong. I thought borrowing all that money was the right move. How did that man find the place when I hadn't been there in a week?" None of this made any sense.

"Really?"

"I was working with Moose and I didn't

want to lead anyone back to the house, so I stayed away."

"How did you hide the paper trail from them?"

"My sister rented it for us. Her name and mine are different." She paused. "He found them there, where they should have been safe."

Jude pulled up at a stoplight. Downtown was busy as usual, foot traffic and cars. Zoe rolled down the window a fraction so she could feel the breeze on her face.

The window rolled back up, and the gust of fresh air stopped.

"I thought you were cold."

She glanced at Jude. "I just wanted to be able to breathe for a minute." That wasn't why she'd opened the window, but now that she'd said that it made sense.

This life, all this danger. The stress of constantly looking over her shoulder had her feeling trapped. Moose had seemed like her way out, but even with new identities she and Tyler would be in danger. Forever looking over their shoulders as they wondered when life would crash around them. Again.

She just wanted to wake up and realize all this was a nightmare. For her life to only be about worrying if Tyler should read more books and watch less TV—the answer was always yes to that question. Life wasn't easy, but it also didn't have to be filled with danger.

If she had the energy, she would pray for an answer. Surely there was something she could do to end this, instead of this being their new reality. Tyler had been through enough upheaval in his life; he didn't need this on top of everything else.

Jude pulled into a parking space at the far end of the lot. Zoe glanced in all directions, out the tinted windows. "Aren't we going to be exposed, walking all the way across the lot to get inside? Shouldn't we park closer to the door?"

Jude shut off the engine. "We're going to be cautious, but we don't know where he is or what his plans are. We could twist ourselves in knots trying to figure out where the attack will come from. It's best to just be smart. Cautious and aware, expecting the danger but not consumed by fear of it."

"I'd love to not be twisted up in knots, but I don't think it's possible to be otherwise right now." She didn't want her voice to sound like that. Zoe fought the frustration and said, "I'm sorry. That was rude. You're helping and I should be more grateful."

"I know you're tired." His soft gaze met hers. "Thank you for apologizing, but it's not necessary. You should be frustrated, because this is a frustrating situation you're caught up in." He touched her shoulder. "I'm not going anywhere."

"Okay, now I feel worse." She gave him a wry smile. "Why can't you be a jerk or something?"

"So you can reinforce your belief that all men are untrustworthy?" He shook his head. "Not on your life."

"Fine."

If he wanted to prove he was a good guy, maybe even *the best guy*, it was fine with her. She was open to being surprised, or even for once being wrong about someone. Logically she knew every guy in the world couldn't be a bad guy. Some of them had to be nice, or no marriage would ever last.

Jude grinned. "Fine." Then cracked his door. "Coffee?"

"I've had four cups already this morning, but the answer to that question is *always* yes."

"So noted." He hopped out. "Wait there until I come around."

She did as he asked, and as they crossed the parking lot she realized he'd slipped into some trained Secret Service agent mode. He was cute when he was all business. But that only made Zoe sigh.

"All right?"

She pushed the diner door open. "Yeah."

Tell that to her heart. It was softening toward him and Zoe didn't know if she could stop it. Even if he really was a good guy, how was that going to help her? She was supposed to be keeping a distance. No one was so good they just helped another person without expecting something in return.

He had to have an angle. Though it didn't make much sense he'd parked them at his parents' instead of in a motel if he was planning on using her for something.

She sat opposite Jude, and they ordered coffee. Zoe got decaf just to prove she could deny herself what she really wanted for her own good. If she couldn't keep her distance with Jude then she was seriously at risk of handing over her heart and having it stomped on.

A shiny muscle car pulled up out front.

"That's them."

Good. Zoe was ready to tell her story and get this part over with so she could figure out how to fix the rest of her life.

She watched out the window as two suited detectives got out of their vehicle. Halfway to the door, shots rang out. A van crawled along the street, the muzzle of a gun pointed out the window.

The cops ducked.

"Get down." Jude leaned over the table and shoved her head down. Seconds later she heard the rev of that muscle car's engine as it drove away. "They went after them." His eyes pinned hers. "Stay here, where you're surrounded by people, but stay down." Jude got up from their booth and raced to the door.

Zoe glanced around, trying to figure out what had just happened.

In that moment, the man she had been running from emerged from the back hallway marked Restrooms. He stared at her, that gleam of evil in his eyes.

He was going to kill her.

SEVEN

Jude raced out the door right into the morning sun. He shaded his eyes with his hand and peered down the street, where the detectives raced in their car after the vehicle of men who had shot at them.

Logic kicked in now. He couldn't go after them. How would that help? The detectives needed space to do their thing, and Jude had to stay with Zoe. To keep her safe no matter what happened.

His stomach churned. He'd left Zoe alone. With a diner full of people, sure. But he hadn't stayed with her.

When the need to keep her safe had become his prime directive, he wasn't sure. Likely sometime during last night, when he'd lain awake wondering why carrying a sleepy child in his arms felt distinctly normal. It should have been strange, helping Tyler from the car to bed, but it hadn't. Nor had sitting with the boy at the kitchen table earlier that morning, eating pancakes and telling funny stories. And that was what struck him the most about this whole situation.

He was supposed to be questioning her, not contemplating whether he might be ready to be a father. Was anyone ever ready?

He'd mostly figured when he had kids then he'd adapt and learn as he went. Now that Zoe and Tyler were suddenly in his life, and he was faced with the strength of Zoe's love for her son, coupled with the fact that Tyler was in as much danger as she was, he had to face realities he'd never contended with before.

He'd never had to keep anyone safe except himself, and he'd been fine living in the narrow world a bachelor dealt with. He'd been content, for now, being friends with the youth kids. Mentoring some of them. Jude didn't even know what it was like to care for someone else that much, but he knew he wanted that in his life.

Romance wasn't on his radar, or it hadn't been until Zoe looked up at him with those big green eyes. That connection was what had been missing from his life so far. *Why now, Lord?* He hadn't prayed for a wife, not yet. Was Zoe, and all her accompanying danger, really what God thought he needed?

Someday, maybe.

Now Jude was facing the fact that all his plans and intentions to wait until after he was established in his career before starting a family weren't necessary. If this was God working in his life then Jude had to refocus everything he'd thought was a priority to make room for it.

Or, maybe it wasn't that cut-and-dried.

Right now, he could do his job *and* protect Zoe. Jude pulled out his phone and called the detective he'd spoken with an hour ago.

"Kind of busy."

Jude didn't much care. Zoe was in danger, and the longer they stayed in one place the greater the chances were that they would be found. "Are you coming back?"

"Backup is delayed. We're taking this."

"You know who these guys are?"

The detective muttered something, then blew out a breath. "Watch it." A second later he said, "No idea who these guys are—never seen them before."

"And they just shot at you, unprovoked?"

"We have no idea why they decided to do it."

Jude looked at the door to the diner. Was this about Zoe? It was possible these guys had been hired to shoot at the two detectives.

Hired to stop them from meeting with Zoe. Hired to stop Zoe from telling the cops what she knew.

The interview was supposed to have been about Moose's murder, but this was something much bigger. How it tied into his investigation, Jude hadn't figured out yet. Zoe might have nothing to do with the money. Then again, she might be smack in the middle of it all.

He needed to keep her close until he figured out which it was.

"Call me later when you want to give this another try."

"Yup." The detective hung up.

Jude made his way back over to the diner. He grabbed the door handle and pulled. The attack against the officers might have been an elaborate distraction. But for what? Energy surged through him. Worry for Zoe and whether she was safe.

She raced out the door he'd just opened and slammed into him. Jude's arms wrapped around her, a reflexive action. She wound her arms around his waist and clung to him, her breath coming fast. Zoe wasn't the kind of woman who easily lost her cool.

"What happened?"

She looked up at him, those green eyes as big

and wide as he'd seen them in the Laundromat. "He was here. The man who killed Moose."

She glanced back, inside the restaurant. "I think he's gone now though. He just stared at me." She shivered.

"Tucker Wilson?" That probably wasn't his name, but Jude didn't know what else to call him.

Zoe nodded, her movements frantic. Her whole body shook. He held her tighter and rubbed one hand up and down her back. Only to help her calm down, not because the hug was nice. This didn't have anything to do with his feelings. It was about helping Zoe.

"Wait here." He set her away from him, just to prove he could let go of her with no problem anytime he wanted to. The "something's missing" feeling hit him square in the chest as the space between them became a void he desperately wanted to eradicate. But he didn't. "I'll go look."

"Give me your keys."

His head jerked in a shake. "For what?" Was she going to drive off and leave him?

"I'm not going to steal a car with government plates." She shot him a dark look. "I don't want to wait out here. I want to wait in the car. Where it's safe."

He pulled out his keys. "Good idea."

He watched her cross the lot. It might give Tucker Wilson time to escape, but he wanted to know Zoe was safe in the car before he went inside. He wasn't about to leave her unprotected again. When she'd gotten in and clicked the locks to secure herself inside, he went in the diner.

All the patrons stared at him as he walked through the restaurant. The silver shield of the Secret Service wasn't something their agency displayed, preferring to go for anonymity instead of spectacle. Too many people would video him if they knew he was a federal agent, leaving Jude handicapped in his ability to do his job. He didn't need that kind of attention until it became necessary.

He searched for Tucker Wilson, but didn't find the man even when he headed out the back door. He circled the building back to the parking lot.

He was halfway across the lot when his phone rang, so he pulled it out. *Dad calling.* Jude swiped to answer the call. "Dad? Is everything okay? Is Tyler all right?"

Nothing but static greeted him.

"Dad?" Jude picked up his pace until he was only a few feet from the car, the engine already running. "Dad, can you hear me?" He looked at the screen to see if he'd been disconnected, but the call was still active.

The Bluetooth icon was on, which meant the call had connected in the car.

Jude was running fast now. Concern for the boy rushed through him, a numbing pain he couldn't think past. If something happened to Tyler, Zoe would be devastated. He didn't know if his parents could handle that kind of responsibility. Who could? No one wanted an innocent to get hurt while under their protection. Jude didn't want that for them, and the last thing he wanted was for the boy to become a casualty of whatever was going on. He would do everything in his power to prevent that from happening.

Zoe gripped the edges of the seat, feeling the hum of the car engine. "I'm okay, Andrew. Are you?"

"We're all okay," Andrew answered. "Right now, at least."

So why had he phoned? As soon as the call had connected in the car, via the Bluetooth, Zoe had felt the ice-cold shock of fear for her son's life.

She'd been on edge since she saw Tucker Wilson inside the diner. His eyes had been as cold as they were in the Laundromat when he'd killed one person and shot another. Had he forced those two detectives away with a diversion in an attempt to kidnap her?

She hadn't waited around to find out. Zoe had simply raced to the front and out the door, where she slammed into Jude. That hug had been the best hug of her life. And while she *knew* she shouldn't get used to relying on him like that, it had certainly felt good at the time. Better than good, actually.

"I think someone might be creeping around outside, though. Where's Jude?"

Zoe glanced out every window of the SUV. "I see him. He's coming over."

She leaned over and unlocked the doors, then cracked the driver's door. His vehicle had been her safe haven more than once since they'd met. The fact that Jude would be here with her as well made it all the more secure.

After weeks of feeling nothing but scared and alone, it was wonderful to know she wasn't alone even if she was still scared.

Jude swung the door wide.

"Your dad is on the phone." She pointed to the center display.

He glanced at it. "Everything okay?"

"He thinks someone is outside their house."

Jude got in and shut his door. "We're on our way."

Zoe buckled her seat belt fast and he did the same before he put the SUV in Drive and pulled out of the lot.

"Tell me what's happening."

"I saw someone outside. A man," Andrew said.

Zoe figured interjecting her own questions wouldn't be helpful. Still, they raced through her head like rows on a spreadsheet. Where was Tyler? Was he okay? Was Andrew *sure* he was okay? Where was Jude's mom? It wouldn't do any good to ask. Until she saw for herself that they were fine, she wouldn't trust it.

That was the reason she had such a hard time with the faith she'd learned about at all those summer camps she'd gone to as a kid. It had been more enjoyable than staying home, where there was no food and nothing on TV. Her mom hadn't been into games or toys, and she was always at work during those endless summer days Zoe had filled with doing whatever her friends did.

That meant Vacation Bible School with a girl who'd lived two doors down. Snacks, games and plenty of other kids to play with. Zoe had loved it, and all the talk about God and Jesus had been interesting. The idea of a heavenly Father being there to protect and guide her was tempting enough that she'd been a believer for a while, but she'd also had to learn to stand on her own two feet. Experience had taught her that she could only rely on herself.

Now Zoe trusted things she could see, things she could prove with evidence. Something she hadn't taken the time to do with God. There was evidence; she'd just never looked into it for herself because she'd been busy. Then she got married, and Tyler had come. After that she was too busy because everything was falling apart. Now wasn't exactly the time to do it, either. She could ask Jude about it, though. It was clear he had come from a family where faith was the norm. What made him retain that belief through adulthood—especially given all the evil he had likely seen during his career as a federal agent?

"We'll be there in ten minutes."

"Okay, I'm looking out the window," Andrew said. "I can't see anyone now. It was just for a second, but I didn't want to take any chances."

Zoe heard him moving around on the other end of the line.

"Leanne went to make sure Tyler was all right." He paused, then called out, "Honey?"

Jude gripped the wheel and drove as fast as was safe through the streets back to the church. She wished he could go faster. How could he be so calm, so focused? Her thoughts were all over the place.

He said, "What's going on, Dad?"

"One second." The phone rustled, then Jude's mom's voice came over the line. "Tyler isn't in his room."

Zoe gasped. "What?"

"Dad!" Panic broke through Jude's unruffled demeanor.

The fact that he cared about her son, and his family, so much was some comfort. But it didn't dispel the terror that moved through her. "It can't be the same guy. He was here, and he didn't have enough time to get back to your house, right?"

Jude nodded, the muscle in his jaw tight. "Dad?"

"Yeah, son?"

"Find Tyler. We'll be there as soon as we can be, okay?"

"We're looking."

"And have Mom call the police. If there is someone outside, and if Tyler is in danger, then we need the cops there to help."

Zoe nodded, pleased he didn't want to act like some lone cowboy and try to do it all himself. Even though she didn't trust the police could do anything to help her, she still wanted them there.

"Good idea, Jude." Then, speaking to Leanne, Andrew said, "Go look in the sanctuary. I'm going to check the youth and children's rooms. And be careful."

Her son was in good hands—or would be, when they found him. Jude was cut from the same cloth. Which didn't make her feel good about herself. She didn't have that kind of role model. Her mom had been self-absorbed at best, and the worse was just that—worse. Zoe had spent years trying to do better, to be a better wife and mom than her own mom had ever been. Her son deserved more than she'd had.

Zoe looked at Jude's hands on the wheel. She wanted him to let go and hold hers, but he was concentrating.

He glanced at her. "We'll be there in a minute."

It would be more like five, but she appreciated his attempt to reassure her. There wasn't much more he could do. Just drive faster. She wanted them to get there in one piece, so she just let him concentrate without having to deal with her, as well.

She couldn't help saying, "Please find him, Andrew."

"I'm looking now." Jude's father's voice was

soft. That was when Jude reached over and squeezed her hand.

"Could he have gone outside?"

She frowned at Jude's question. "Yes, if he thought it was the right thing to do. He knows that if he thinks he's in danger, he's supposed to make himself safe, and then wait for help to come to him."

"I can check outside," Andrew said. "But we'll finish looking inside first."

"Good idea," Jude told his dad. Then he said, "They have to rule out inside first."

She nodded, though the mom in her wanted to panic at the idea that her son was in danger. "Hurry, please." He couldn't drive faster, but she needed to say it anyway.

"Hang on," Andrew said. "What is it, Leanne?"

Jude's mom's voice came over the line. "I saw the man again, and he has a ski mask on. He's outside, by the trees. And Tyler isn't in here."

Zoe's stomach rolled over like she'd eaten bad shrimp. "The tree house."

EIGHT

Zoe was out of the car before he'd even come to a complete stop. *Again*. Jude shut off the engine and ran after her as she circled the building. He caught up in time to open the gate before she attempted to scale the fence.

She moved to go first, but Jude held her back with his arm. He palmed his weapon and said, "Stay behind me."

The last thing he needed was for her to become a casualty of whatever was happening. Really, he should have made her wait in the car, but having her with him meant he would at least be able to keep an eye on her.

Jude made his way to the rear of the building. If Tyler had gone to the tree house, he'd have come out the back door. But it wasn't Tyler he found there.

"Dad!" Jude rushed to where his father lay on the grass beside the walking path. After he scanned the whole area and saw no one he fell to his knees at his dad's side. A gash on his forehead trickled blood down his face in a stream. Jude pulled out the handkerchief his dad always kept in his left pocket and balled it up before pressing it to his father's forehead.

Zoe set her hand on his shoulder and leaned down to ask his father, "Where's Tyler?"

His dad moaned and opened his eyes for a second. His vision was glassy. Was it just a concussion, or something even more serious? "Dad, can you hear me?"

Jude's mom raced from the house carrying a first-aid kit. "Your father told me to wait inside. When he came out, someone sneaked up behind him. They must not have seen me—" she wrung her hands together "—when I yelled to your father, he turned and whoever it was clocked him on the head." Tears rolled down his mother's face. "It's all my fault, Jude."

Jude pulled out gauze. "Did you see where Tyler went?" Zoe squeezed his shoulder, whether in thanks or for another reason, he didn't know.

His mom shook her head. "Andrew was going to search for him. That's when I saw the person who attacked him."

Zoe said, "I'm going to check the tree house."

Jude nodded. She would be within view the whole time, which was the only reason he let her go look for Tyler by herself. Jude pulled out his phone and called 9-1-1, explaining who he was. The police were on their way due to his mother's earlier call. Now they would send an ambulance, as well.

Jude ended the call and pocketed his phone, but he couldn't relax. He could barely pull in a full breath as fear over what could've happened rolled through him.

His father could so easily have been killed. Tyler could still be missing—he might not be in the tree house—and then what would they do? Zoe would be distraught. And Tyler…what would happen to him in these killers' hands?

He started to pray.

Seconds later Zoe emerged from the tree house, followed by Tyler. Jude blew out the breath he'd been holding, then scanned the area again as they climbed down the rungs nailed to the tree trunk.

"He looks okay."

His mom nodded. She settled onto the grass across from him, his father between them. "You care about them."

"Of course."

"I mean, more than one human being cares simply because another human being is in danger. I mean you *care*."

Jude shrugged. He hadn't examined his feelings more than that. There had hardly been any time to. "I haven't known them long enough to know if that's true. Zoe seems like a nice woman in a seriously tough spot, and Tyler is in danger, as well. Zoe's sister was nearly killed." They needed to visit her in the hospital, as they'd told Tyler he could. The boy needed to see for himself that his aunt was mending—assuming she hadn't taken a turn for the worse.

"Beyond that?" Jude shrugged. "Why don't we just worry about what's happening in the moment instead of what may or may not happen in the future?" After all, he had to find out what Zoe knew about BioWell. Not dig into his feelings.

Her eyebrows lifted. "You're thinking about the future?"

"Mom."

"What?" She spread her hands, all innocence, then looked at his father and winced. "Is your father going to be okay?"

"The ambulance will be here soon." Jude prayed some more.

"He hit him so hard." She swallowed, as though just the memory of it made her sick.

Zoe and Tyler clung to each other as they walked across the grass. Jude scanned the area looking for his father's assailant, then let his gaze land on Tyler.

The boy didn't look injured, which was good. It was just Jude's father who was hurt. Dad wouldn't have had it any other way. That was the value system he'd instilled in Jude— to risk even his own life if it meant shielding the people under his protection. It was mostly the reason why Jude had become a federal agent. Protecting people was what he wanted to do every day. Fighting against criminals who hurt innocent people, and helping to make the world safer. His work was important. Not more or less than dad and his ministry, just different.

It was the path Jude had chosen for himself. And he believed that in order to achieve it, he'd have to put off some of the other things he'd wanted. If Zoe and Tyler had been put in his path by God, perhaps he had been wrong about that.

Maybe God wanted to give him *everything* he wanted. But why now? This was hardly the right time.

"Tell me what the person looked like."

His mom's brows crinkled, but she didn't stop stroking her husband's hand, which she was holding in hers. "Short, I think. Like my height. He was shorter than your father. Dark blue coat and dark pants. Slender, but the clothes were baggy. A hood covered his head."

"Not a ski mask?"

She shook her head.

Jude didn't think it could've been Tucker Wilson. The description didn't match, and there wasn't enough time for him to have been at the diner, and then get to the church to terrorize them and hurt his father. But that just brought more questions, since it meant Tucker Wilson was definitely working with someone else. Just as he'd considered after the fire.

"I never saw his face. I didn't get a real good look at him."

"That's okay, Mom." Jude heard the siren of the first police car. He waited with his dad while the officers secured the scene, content to let them take over. Finally the EMTs arrived and loaded his dad onto their vehicle.

"Do you need to get checked out, Tyler?"

When the boy didn't say anything, Jude looked at Zoe. She said, "I think he's okay. Just freaked out."

Jude nodded. He walked across the grass with his mom, helped her into the ambulance so she could go with his father and made sure she had her purse to take with her, as well.

"Thank you, Jude."

He nodded, the lump in his throat too big to answer her. The ambulance drove away and he turned back to find Zoe and Tyler had followed him across the grass. They were right behind him so that when he turned they were close enough to pull into his arms.

"Is he dead?"

Jude leaned back and looked down at Tyler's face. "No. He isn't dead. I'm so sorry you thought that. He's hurt right now, but he's going to be fine." He sighed. "The man who was here hit him in the head. Did you see him?"

Zoe stiffened, but he ignored her reaction and focused on Tyler. She was probably just worried for her son and the fact that he'd had to hide from an attacker.

Tyler said, "I didn't know he hit Mr. Andrew. But I saw him afterward. And the other one."

Two people? "Do you know who they were?"

"They had masks on."

Zoe exhaled. Jude couldn't help wondering if she was relieved or disappointed Tyler didn't know who the man was. Or glad Tyler couldn't be called as a witness.

Tyler said, "And he told me to give Mom a message."

* * *

Zoe lifted her chin and addressed the officer. "Yes, I left the Laundromat before you got there. It isn't that I didn't want to give you my statement. I feared for my life." Among other things. Because, really, the killer had left before she did. She hadn't expected him to be waiting for her. But she had been afraid.

The officer didn't look happy, but he also didn't attempt to infringe on what she knew were her rights as a witness to not be involved. She didn't *have* to tell them anything. And while part of that was self-preservation, most of it was the fact that she still didn't believe they could help her.

Zoe glanced at him then, crouched down in front of her son. It could have been a sweet moment between them if it weren't for the fact that she knew he was probably asking Tyler about the message and the man who had given it to him—and the *other* person. Zoe wanted to go over and listen to what they were discussing, but the officer wanted her accounting of events and Jude had encouraged her to give her statement.

"Are we done?" If they were, she would head straightaway toward Tyler and Jude.

The officer studied her face, then sighed. "Stay safe."

Zoe frowned at that, but he walked away. As though he hadn't meant anything by those words. She shook off the thought and headed for Jude and her son. The Secret Service agent was listening to Tyler, who broke off what he'd been saying when she walked over and looked up at her.

Zoe smiled and pulled him to her side in a hug. Tyler pressed his face against her middle. "Pretty soon you're going to be head-butting my shoulder when you do that." She ruffled his hair and he leaned back with a smile on his face.

"Then I'll be messing up your hair."

Zoe smiled. "You can try." Jude straightened and she glanced at him. "Everything okay?"

"Tyler was just about to tell me what the man said."

She frowned. Hadn't they been talking about him that whole time?

"We wanted to wait for you."

"Oh." She held her son's hand. "What happened, Ty?"

"I was in the tree house."

He paused, so Zoe said, "That's good. I want you to do what you need to do to make sure that you're safe, okay? Adults can help protect you, if you know them and you trust them. Like Ember and Jude, and his parents."

"Is Mr. Andrew okay?"

"We can go to the hospital and find out," Jude said. "But first, will you tell me what happened in the tree house?"

Tyler nodded. "I was hiding in there and I heard someone climb up. I thought it was Mr. Andrew." He chewed his lip this time, his hand trembling in Zoe's. She hated that her son was so scared. How was she going to figure this out now? Maybe Jude knew what she should do.

Tyler said, "The man…he had a peeling nose."

"Like a sunburn?" Jude asked.

Tyler nodded. Zoe figured her son had seen her boss, but didn't look at Jude when he glanced at her. He didn't need to see it written on her face that she could guess who the man was.

"He smiled, but it was mean. And he said, 'Found you.' Then he told me to tell you that you should tell the feds everything you know. He said it was the only way he would be free."

Zoe's stomach knotted. With Moose gone and no ID's, how could they start a new life? She would have liked to just run with her son, be safe and never come back. Now she was tangled up with Jude and the Secret Service of all things. Were they the answer?

This man wanted her to stay, to put her son in danger? Zoe didn't know if she wanted to go into witness protection, but disappearing sounded better every day. It was what she'd planned all along.

She hugged Tyler again, just so thankful he was all right. The man could have hurt or even killed him as a warning, or out of hatred for her. The fact that her baby was alive still was a blessing she was never going to take for granted.

"What about the other one you saw?"

Tyler shrugged, and Jude leaned down. He put his hand on Tyler's shoulder. "You were very brave. I know federal agents who couldn't face down a bad guy the way you did."

Zoe didn't know if that was exactly true, but it seemed to make Tyler feel better. The only thing that would make her feel better right now would be if they grabbed their stuff and got out of there.

Jude's voice interrupted her thoughts. "Whatever you're thinking, I feel like I'm not going to like it."

She glanced at him. "He wants me to stay? I'm not going to do that."

"You're just going to take off?"

"I don't believe we'll be safe if we stay. So, yes. Of course. Why would I *not* do the opposite of what he wants? It's probably a trap."

She wasn't to believe anything Alan Reskin said. A murderer couldn't be trusted—if that was who had spoken with Tyler.

He did look kind of disappointed. "You'll run, instead of fighting?"

"Your dad is in the hospital, Jude. And my sister. Who will be next? You? Tyler?" She shook her head. "There's no way I'm going to let that happen when I have the power to prevent it."

"Where will you go?"

"Does it matter?"

He blew out a breath. "This doesn't make you guys safe."

She said nothing. Jude was safer this way, and she was not about to risk yet another person's life when she had the answer now. They didn't even have to pack, because everything had burned and she still had her money. If she wasn't buying ID's from Moose, she needed to give it back. She'd still owe interest, but it was the fastest way to pay off that debt.

"Is there something you need me for? Because I'd like to leave now." She heard the coldness in her voice, the tone she'd used with the detective she hadn't wanted to talk to.

"I'm trying to figure out why this man is making contact, telling you to spill all when he sent Tucker after you. He's undermining whatever he had set in motion."

"Maybe he changed his mind. Or he's going against someone else." What was Reskin thinking?

"Or Tucker went rogue. Maybe he's out of control." Jude's jaw was a hard line. "The second person could be the one he wants to escape from."

"Okay." She didn't really know why that was so important. Besides, it seemed like he was brainstorming or something. "So?"

"So it means, even if you do what the old man told you and testify, good ole Tucker still might not back down." Jude glanced at Tyler, then pinned her with a stare. "You could be in danger from him if you follow the message instructions."

"That's why we're leaving!"

Jude glanced at the retreating cop cars. "I want to go check on my dad. Will you come?"

"I want to check on my sister as well, but as soon as that's done we're *gone*."

He waited while she went inside, and they

piled into his SUV in silence. What was she supposed to say? She knew Jude wanted her to stay and fight this. Maybe if she didn't have Tyler, she would have. But it wasn't just her life on the line. She had a son to think about.

Maybe if Ember had been okay, Zoe could have sent Tyler away with her. A monthlong vacation until all this blew over. That would have been good, though she had no idea how they'd have paid for it. Other than the thirty-thousand she'd borrowed.

Would the federal government keep Ember safe as well if Zoe and Tyler went into witness protection? She could testify knowing all of her family was safe.

Jude made a noise, low in his throat, his gaze on the rearview.

"What?" She was in the back with Tyler, but leaned forward. "What is it?"

He didn't say anything, just kept driving. Zoe looked out the back window, where a black-and-white cop car tailed them. "We have an escort?"

"I guess," he said. "Though no one told me about it."

Zoe didn't worry about it, since she had plenty of other problems to occupy her thoughts. At least, she didn't worry about it until the police car lights came on and the siren sounded for a second. "Is he pulling us over?"

"Yes," Jude said. "The question is, why?"

NINE

Jude glanced at Zoe in the backseat, her son huddled against her body. The cops hadn't said anything to him earlier about a protection detail, and now they were pulling him over?

Jude hit his turn signal and moved to the shoulder on the side of the street. They were miles from their destination, and his father was probably being stitched up already. Even though his mom was with him didn't mean Jude didn't want to be there, as well. Despite the differences between him and his father, they were still close.

Jude peered at the driver in the cop car. Did he know this man? He was familiar with a few of the local officers, but they were at the far end of the city. The ones who patrolled downtown were different officers from a different precinct—not the same ones who would have responded to a call to his dad's church.

Jude pulled to a stop under the giant bough

of a tree that hung over the shoulder. They were still a ways from the hospital. Traffic was light here. He ran down all his options while he listened to the rustle of Zoe's clothing in the backseat, not liking the timing of this.

Jude snapped the clasp on his weapon holster.

The driver's door of the police cruiser opened and a slender man unfolded himself from the seat. Was any cop that skinny? Certainly many were lean, but this man looked almost emaciated—like he'd foregone eating in favor of consuming drugs one too many times.

Jude recognized him, and the man was no cop. Did his eyes shine with the gleam of a high as they had in the Laundromat, when Jude had shot him in the chest?

Something wasn't right.

Jude pulled his phone from the cup holder and sent a quick SOS text to the task force on-call phone. Just to be safe.

If there was ever a time to reach out for help it was when he had not one but two innocents in his backseat.

Ice-cold fingertips brushed the back of his neck. Milsner might not think Jude was doing the right thing, but he still had to follow his instincts. There was no way Jude would let Zoe just leave. He understood her reasoning, but how would she ever be safe if she ran?

The response from the duty agent was immediate.

Copy that.

He was too tall to have been the person his mom had seen. The idea it could, in fact, have been a woman who'd hit his father was something he contemplated—but not for long. One more person to find. After this was done. The fact that there were actually three people looking for Zoe was something he had no time to worry about right now.

Zoe's voice came from the backseat. "Is that…?"

"Yes."

He didn't like the high vibrato of her voice, when it was normally a steady alto. Jude twisted to look around the headrest at Tyler. He locked eyes with the boy. "I've got this. Okay?"

Tyler said nothing. Did nothing.

"I've got this, Tyler. Backup is on the way. You understand me?"

There was a reason why Jude was here with them. There *had* to be. Only God could have orchestrated this so that it was Jude, the federal agent, who was here to face down the threat to them. The alternative didn't even

bear thinking about. It made him shudder as
he pushed from his mind the image of Tyler,
hurt. Or Zoe, bleeding on the side of the road.

There was no way Jude would let that happen.

The "officer" loped toward them. Anyone
driving by would think this was a normal traffic stop.

He could hit the gas right now. Drive away,
get Zoe and Tyler to safety. This was an opportunity to end the running and face down
Tucker. But not with his two passengers in
danger.

Jude gripped the door handle, praying
the man would go down without a fight. He
thumbed the button and the window whirred
down so he could shoot through the open window if he needed to. He could slam the door
into Tucker Wilson when he got close enough.
Jude needed all those options open, because
there was no way Tucker would come quietly
even if he gave the man that option.

"Zoe." Jude didn't turn around.

"What?"

"The moment I get out of the car do you
think you can climb in the front seat?" He
didn't like the idea of her out of his sight, but
the SUV had a GPS tracker. "Drive. Doesn't
matter where, just go."

The cop unsnapped his gun as he walked up to the back quarter panel.

A red stain on this pretend cop's shirt made him grit his teeth. A hole left by a bullet. Jude choked the lump in his throat back down.

Where was the officer this man had shot? Shot, and then stripped of his clothes. Was the dead cop another casualty of whatever had caused the CEO of BioWell to murder a woman?

"When this is done," Jude said in a low tone, "as soon as we get the chance, you're going to tell me exactly what you know about Alan Reskin's business."

She cleared her throat. "Okay, Jude. Fine. Just…okay."

Good. He was glad she understood what was happening here. Jude couldn't protect her if she didn't tell him everything. And that meant *everything*. This would never end if she didn't give him the tools he needed—information—to end it.

Tucker Wilson—or whatever his name was—stood beside the driver's door of Jude's SUV, two feet back so he was out of Jude's reach. "Out of the car." His voice quavered, but not from fear. Jude figured it had more to do with the high of snapping a trap closed and facing down his prey.

Jude had his engine still running so Zoe could get away. He reached for the handle to get out.

"Not so fast." The killer pulled the weapon from his holster. "Hands where I can see them."

Jude wanted to ask who the man with the message for Tyler had been, but couldn't begin his line of questioning until they were in the interrogation room. Bringing it up now would only antagonize him into using his weapon. Instead, he said, "I'm getting out. Let's talk."

"Not you," he said to Jude, then waved at the backseat. "Them." A pause. "I'll take the woman. You can keep the kid, unless she does something I don't like. In that case, he's dead and I still take her."

In the backseat, Tyler sucked back a sob. Or was that Zoe?

Did it matter? Jude wasn't going to let *any-thing* happen to them. Not when it felt like his life had started since he'd met Zoe.

Zoe clutched Tyler to her. She should have moved him the minute they were pulled over, put her son behind her so that he was shielded. Could it have made a difference? Her body wouldn't give him much protection. Didn't most bullets just punch through the person and hit whatever was behind? She didn't want to be the real-life example of that.

Either way, she couldn't do anything to prevent it if this guy really wanted to hurt Tyler. She didn't have body armor—for either of them. And she didn't have the weapons or skills to save them in a fight. Only Jude could do that, and he wanted her to drive away.

A shudder moved through her. Tucker was willing to kill Tyler just to get her to go with him. The idea scared her to death.

"Move by me, baby." As soon as she had Tyler's attention she started to shift his body. When he caught her meaning, he climbed over her lap so she was between the gunman and her son. Instead of nothing.

Jude couldn't get out. Zoe had to do something.

She cracked the door. "Tyler, stay here."

"Zoe." Jude cracked his door, too.

She climbed out, and he did the same. She couldn't meet his eyes, though. She was supposed to be driving away. There was no way she could do that if it meant Tucker shot Jude.

She shut the car door so Tyler stayed put, then lifted her chin and faced down the gunman. Even though doing it made her whole body jerk. She locked her knees and ignored it. "I'll go with you."

When the alternative was Tyler dead? No question.

Jude moved in front of her, his gun ready. "No way." His body was taut, and she wanted to grasp the shirt at his waist and cling to him, to his strength, but what was the point in doing that? It wouldn't get any of them out of danger. She couldn't stand the thought of Jude getting hurt, either.

"Yes." She tried to shove him but he wouldn't move. Strength or stubbornness, she didn't know which but the result was the same. "Jude, get out of my way." She met the gunman's gaze over his shoulder, and said, "I'm going with you. Don't hurt them."

"If you think he'll keep that promise," Jude said, "then you're going to be disappointed when he proves you wrong. And he *will* prove you wrong. I have no doubt in my mind about that."

Why did that matter? She had to try. Didn't he understand that?

She stared at their attacker. "Take me with you."

His gaze narrowed. "Your fed here needs to stand down."

"Jude." She didn't want to leave him, not

like this. But there was no other choice. She was getting entirely too attached to Jude Brauer. This was the better way. She would give this man what he wanted, and Jude could keep Tyler safe.

"No." He was unmoving.

Gun faced down against gun. The only difference was that one man was sane, and the other was completely unhinged.

Tucker Wilson lifted his gun and pointed it at Jude. The Secret Service agent did the same. "Move. She goes with me, and you walk away with the kid."

Jude shook his head. He took a step back, so that she pressed against the SUV. Zoe darted to the side. Jude tried to grasp her arm but she got out of reach. Now he was protecting Tyler, which was what she wanted anyway.

Why did it feel like a loss?

She wanted to cry at the look of betrayal on Jude's face, but she moved…not closer to the crazy gunman. She couldn't bring herself to do that. Instead, she stepped away from both of them. Now that she'd committed to going with him, she was wavering.

"Zoe." Jude looked and sounded mad. She could tell he didn't like this at all. Well, neither did she, but she was taking the power back.

She shook her head and stood her ground.

The gunman moved to her and grabbed her arm. In a second she would be in his car and… He didn't take her toward the car. No, he hauled her to the trees. She struggled. "What are you—"

"Shut up." He didn't slow down, not even when Zoe tripped over her feet. "We're ending this. No more messing around, no mind games. It's done."

Dread settled, cold in her stomach. She wanted to look back, to see Tyler's face in the car window. To see the love, and feel what was between them. Motherhood had given her so much and she was about to lose it all. *God help me.* She needed all the help she could get right now.

The gunman held his weapon pointed at Jude, making sure he didn't come over and try to help her. Within minutes they were deep in the trees, an overgrown part of the park. No one else was here.

"Where are—"

"I said, shut up." He gripped her arm until she was sure he would leave bruises when he was done.

More images flashed through her mind, and she saw herself laid out on a metal table ready to be autopsied. What would the medical examiner say about her? *She put up a fight.* That would be the strong thing to do.

Zoe looked around for something to use as a weapon, but she knew nothing about weapons. And the only thing she knew about nature was that it was usually itchy. She much preferred her air-conditioned gym.

He hauled her in front of him and lifted his gun.

Zoe stared down the barrel and a sob caught in her throat. Tears rolled down her face. "I didn't see anything." Okay, that was a lie, but it was the first thing that had come to mind. "She looked dead, but it's not like I checked—maybe she was just unconscious. He was standing over her, and I assumed he killed her but I don't know that. I could be mistaken."

She wanted to laugh through the sob. She was going crazy, seconds before she was going to die.

He grinned, more of a sneer. "Wrong place, seriously wrong time. And you just couldn't let it lie. Well, turns out neither can they."

"I won't say anything. I promise."

"Too late. You've drawn attention to yourself. Now she's convinced you'll blab, and that can't happen. So instead of taking you to her I'm ending this. No more scare tactics. No more threats. Problem solved."

She? So there was someone involved other than just Alan Reskin. She didn't know who— but now wasn't the time to find out. Zoe ran as fast as she could.

A shot rang out.

Pain tore through her shoulder and Zoe hit the ground.

TEN

Tucker stumbled to one knee and clutched his thigh where Jude had shot him. Jude ran to crouch by Zoe, his gaze—and the aim of his weapon—still pointed squarely at Tucker Wilson. "Put your gun down."

He'd caught up to them not long before the man opened fire on her. Jude had no choice but to intervene.

The guy moaned but complied, using his other hand to add pressure to his leg. Jude pressed his fingers to Zoe's neck. A cold breeze through the trees cut to his bones as adrenaline dissipated, leaving shock in its wake. Her skin was warm under his fingertips and he breathed a sigh. The bullet had hit her shoulder, but she was out cold. Had she slammed her head when she fell?

He didn't want to leave her, but he needed to grab the man's gun so it was out of his grasp. Her assailant grimaced, but didn't attempt to run. Still, Jude said, "Don't even think about trying anything."

He went back over to Zoe and pulled out his phone to call for an ambulance. Reality blew through him like a cold breeze, which wouldn't let up. First her stepsister, Ember, then his father and now Zoe. The man in front of him had caused so much destruction, but now at least this part was done.

Zoe moaned. She began to shift, so he said, "Try to lie still. The ambulance is on its way."

He felt more than heard her nod. Jude smoothed back hair from her face, keeping part of his attention on the man. "Everything is going to be okay. I got him, and he can't hurt you."

"Jude!"

At the yell, he looked up. Three members of the task force ran toward him, guns drawn. Milsner was in the lead.

Jude hadn't even had time to don his vest like these guys had. *Thank You for protecting me, Lord.* Zoe had been hurt, but it could have been so much worse—for both of them.

"Hey, guys. I'm glad you're here." Wasn't that the understatement of the century? He couldn't arrest the gunman and get Zoe to the hospital by himself. Not to mention the gunman needed medical attention, as well. "Did you see a boy in my car?"

Milsner nodded, holding aim on the gunman while another of his coworkers put on the cuffs. "Fronter stayed with him. Kid was pretty freaked out."

"His name is Tyler." Jude was glad to hear he'd stayed put, but regretted the fact that Tyler had been pulled into this in the first place. The little guy had to be so scared, hearing gunshots and not knowing what had happened. He would need someone with him while his mom was patched up at the hospital. "This is his mom, Zoe."

Her eyes were open now, and he could focus on her without having to worry about what Tucker would do. He shifted and leaned closer to her. "Hey, how are you feeling?"

She winced. "Hurts."

"I know. Tyler is good, and an ambulance is on its way for you and for Tucker. We caught him." Something darkened her eyes, and he figured he knew what it was. "This isn't over, but you aren't in danger from him now. He can't hurt you from jail."

She nodded, a tiny movement that seemed full of pain.

"Ambulance is here."

It felt like forever before the first set of EMTs patched up Tucker well enough to take him to the hospital. Agent Milsner and Agent

Carnes would ride along to make sure the gunman was secure. Zoe was hauled up by the second set of EMTs onto a stretcher. As they trundled to the ambulance she would ride in, he walked behind them. As soon as the SUV came into view Tyler jumped from the open back door.

Agent Fronter yelled, "Hey, kid!" but Jude waved him off. Jude caught up so he was beside Zoe right when Tyler got there, and the kid nearly body slammed him. The EMTs didn't stop.

Jude said, "She was shot in the shoulder, but it isn't bad."

One EMT shot him a frown. What, he shouldn't have told the kid that? Tyler needed the truth, especially when it was his mom who was hurt. They walked with her, Tyler walking sideways so he could touch his mom's arm.

"Is she okay?" His pleading eyes moved to stare up at Jude and he grabbed Jude's hand. He probably needed the reassurance of physical touch.

Jude nodded, all thoughts in his brain eclipsed by the feel of those tiny fingers in his hand. This kid had been through so much, and he was still holding it together. Once Zoe was taken care of Jude needed to take him to see his aunt so he could see for himself that she was healing in the hospital.

Tyler glanced at his mom. One of his sneakers hit a tree branch and he stumbled into Jude. Jude swung the boy up onto his hip, but Tyler crawled around Jude like he was a climbing wall until he was in a piggyback ride. Jude locked his wrists behind his back so the kid had something to sit on and Tyler leaned his cheek on Jude's left shoulder, probably so he could see his mom.

As they moved closer to the ambulance it didn't go unnoticed by the other task force members that Jude carried a child on his back. They knew he was getting to know Zoe, but maybe they hadn't read his report closely enough to know she had a son. Or they were simply surprised he was so close with them after such a short time.

"Is my mom really okay?"

Jude set Tyler on the ground and crouched. "She's hurt, and that's going to last a few weeks. But she'll be a lot better after the doctors see her."

Tyler's mouth twisted, like he was holding back the need to cry. Jude pulled him into a hug. "We'll go with her, okay? Ride in the ambulance."

Tyler nodded against his chest and again

Jude's thoughts were eclipsed by the feel of it. Was this how every parent felt? He didn't get many hugs doing youth ministry, as most of the kids were much older than Tyler. It felt equally strange as it did good.

"Tyler." Zoe's voice was low, but the kid heard it.

Jude nodded. "Go."

The boy ran to where the EMTs were loading her into the ambulance. Jude met Agent Fronter, the man who had waited with Tyler. He held out his hand. "Thank you."

Fronter nodded and shook it. "Sure thing. We'll make sure the suspect is seen to at the hospital, and then get started on the interview. Unless you want us to wait for you?"

Jude shook his head. "You guys go ahead. You don't need me." They were perfectly capable of doing the job without him. Jude was needed with Tyler and Zoe. "I still haven't gotten to check on my father so it'll be a while before I can come in."

His mom could probably watch Tyler if he needed to go to the office. Or maybe he would take the boy with him, to keep him safe. Tyler would probably get a kick out of seeing the inside of the field office.

The man nodded. "We'll keep you posted."

In the meantime Zoe needed to get patched

up and on the road to recovery because Jude had some serious questions to ask her. She had promised she would finally tell him everything and he intended on making sure she kept that promise. The two assailants from the church were still out there, and Zoe and Tyler still weren't safe. This wasn't over.

Jude had a lot of work to do before it was.

Zoe winced, though there wasn't much pain. She was too numb for that. The doctor didn't apologize; he just huffed a laugh. "All in your head."

"That giant needle you stuck in me was *not* in my head."

He grinned, still unapologetic. He was kind of cute, and younger than her, so it was endearing. Not nearly as good-looking as Jude, though. The doctor almost reminded her of Tyler, the time when he'd made her a "cake" out of mud and he'd been so proud of his creation.

"Couple minutes and you'll be good as new."

He'd already stitched the front. Now he was closing the spot on her back where the bullet had exited. Apparently having an exit wound was a good thing, though it didn't feel that way. Her head swam at just the thought of the pain she'd felt lying on the ground. The only good thing had been Jude's face right in front of her, talking in that calm-in-a-crisis voice of his.

Now all she had was major discomfort— thank you, modern medicine—and no Jude. Where was he anyway? He'd disappeared with Tyler right before they cut off her shirt, whispering something about chips and candy bars. Her son would be delighted. But what about her?

Maybe he thought taking Tyler away was helping her. And yes, her son didn't need to see the gruesome extent of her injury. As it was, she was going to have nightmares for months. She didn't need Tyler having them, as well.

Still, tell that to her heart.

"Whoa, you got all sad." The doctor leaned back so she could see his face over her shoulder. "Wanna talk about it?"

She shook her head, sick of people commenting on her being sad. Her life was her life, and she was dealing with it. Thankfully she was saved from any further pestering when Jude walked in. No knock. He simply strode in like he had every right to be here. Worse, she didn't even mind the assumption he was welcome wherever she was. That was going to be a hard feeling to shake when this was all over. For both of them.

His eyes narrowed, and he regarded the doctor with suspicion. "Everything okay?"

The doctor lifted both hands, which gave her a look at that *giant* sewing needle he was using to stitch her up like she was a quilt or something. "Hey, man. It wasn't me." He paused. "I'm actually thinking it was you."

"Me?" Jude angled his finger toward the button-down shirt he was wearing. "What did I do?"

"Guess you'd better ask your lady."

Zoe rolled her eyes. "You don't need to ask me." She glanced back at the doctor. "*He* didn't do anything."

"You hold grudges. First the needle. Now this." He blew out a breath, exasperated. She also got the feeling he was trying to lighten the mood. Maybe it was part of his bedside manner. The doctor stood, tossing the tools of his torture on the tray with a clang. "All done. I'll send the nurse in with your discharge information and a prescription. Okeydokey?"

Zoe nodded, not quite sure what to make of the man.

Jude shook his hand before he left, then

made his way over to her. Before he could say anything she asked, "Where's Tyler?"

"I asked my mom to take him to see your sister. She needed the walk, and he said he wanted to. There's a cop with them. The doctor said Ember is awake and that she was asking for you both."

Zoe hopped off the bed, turned her back and pulled her sweater up from where it hung down behind her back. She lifted it over her shoulder before zipping it up. It had done fine to cover her while the doctor worked. Now she'd have to make do as she didn't have a shirt. She needed clean clothes.

When she turned back to him he smiled gently. "Okay?"

Zoe sat back on the bed with a sigh. "Don't ask me to face down any more gunmen or do anything except nap, and I'll be fine." Jude's look darkened in a way she didn't like at all. So much for being able to take a nap. "What?"

He sat beside her on the bed. So he didn't have to look at her? "When we were in the car, you said you'd tell me everything you know about Alan Reskin's business. I need you to tell me if this is related to the investigation the task force is currently involved in, or something else."

"I don't know if I can answer that ques-

tion." She paused. "I already told you what...
what I saw. But I don't know why he killed
that woman. Or if it has to do with Moose and
whatever you're investigating."

"I'm investigating BioWell Pharmaceuticals." She gasped, but he spoke over it. "I can't
keep the team on your case if it isn't work related. I'll still protect you, of course."

"You just won't be doing it with help?"

He nodded.

And yet he'd go out of his way—risk his
life—to make sure she and Tyler were safe?
"Thank you, Jude. I didn't want to need your
help, but it's been wonderful to feel like someone has my back. I'm so glad it's you."

He nodded. "There's something I need to
tell you, though."

Zoe sucked in a breath, but refused to give
in to her instinct to pull away. She simply had
to be brave. Trust this man who had proved
himself so trustworthy.

He reached over and took her hand in his.
"Your sister told the police something before
she asked for Tyler."

Zoe frowned. "What?"

"The person who set the fire. Ember claims
it was a woman outside your house."

Zoe gasped. "How is that possible? I mean,

I saw a woman—" She realized then. "Tucker said *she*. Right before he shot me."

Jude said nothing, but his look spoke loudly enough.

"But who could it be? The only woman I know who has been part of this was dead. The threatening emails started the next day. I'd called in sick anyway, because I was just so freaked out. It got worse and worse over the next week, until—"

The door opened and Tyler raced inside. He stopped short at the sight of the two of them sitting together on the bed. Jude's mom, following behind him, simply smiled. "Hello, you two."

"Mom?" Tyler said.

Zoe smiled at her son. "I'm all patched up and ready to go home."

Jude hadn't moved on from their conversation, though. "What about the woman? Any other ideas who she could be?"

She looked up at him. Questions like that probably made him a great federal agent, but they made her want to squirm. "I don't know and I don't *want* to know. Thank you for catching Tucker, but I'm still leaving town. There's no reason for us to stay. Not when both Alan Reskin *and* a woman are after me."

Zoe had too many questions and not nearly

enough answers. But she didn't need answers to be safe, right? She had her son. She could make them safe herself.

"Zoe—"

Tyler watched as she stared down Jude. But she couldn't waylay her son's fears right now. "I have no idea what all is going on, but it doesn't matter. Because if I stay to find out, then the only option is to continue to be a target. To let Tyler be a target."

She paused, knowing he didn't like it. "I won't let that happen, Jude. We have a better chance if we run."

ELEVEN

It had been underhanded, but Jude felt no remorse over utilizing her son to get Zoe into the Secret Service office. What kid wouldn't want to take the tour from a real Secret Service agent? So, yeah, he'd sold it like that even though technically it wasn't possible for security reasons. He still needed a statement from her, even if she was going to leave right after. This was work. Not a field trip for Tyler.

The boy walked ahead of Jude and Zoe into the lobby. "Whoa."

Jude chuckled. "Pretty cool, huh." He glanced at Zoe and it became immediately apparent that she didn't share her son's amazement. "Okay?"

Her throat worked as she swallowed. "I guess. Just make this quick."

He wondered what she had to be nervous about here, considering this might just be top of the list of safest places to be in Salt Lake

City. The idea she might feel threatened here was crazy, but she'd been in hiding so he supposed it was understandable. No doubt the longer they were here, the more she'd get the chance to shore up her confidence. And realize the Secret Service, or any federal agent really, posed no threat to her well-being.

He had to stay neutral. She could just be nervous about telling the whole story in an official setting. Zoe hadn't asked to be a witness to a possible murder, and he needed to be professional but also compassionate. And that was so much harder when he actually cared about the witness on a personal level.

She said, "The cops are here?"

Beyond Zoe, Tyler had moved to her side and now held his mom's hand. The detectives who had planned to meet them in the diner were ahead of them, already through the comprehensive security process.

Jude nodded. "As the investigating officers on the murder case, we asked them to conduct their questioning here so they can also obtain the information they need. Crime is rarely cut-and-dried, but it isn't often the police or FBI and Secret Service work this closely. We are on this, though. If BioWell is involved in what we think they are, this could potentially be huge."

"I guess I'm just special, then," she said with a wry smile. "But isn't it *your* case?"

He shrugged. "It's a task force. Your thing is part of it, but only a small part. We have to figure out if your side of the puzzle is the edge, the bottom or the middle."

"So I'm mixed up in a five-thousand-piece puzzle?"

"Could be just fifty pieces. Or you could be part of a different puzzle altogether." He smiled. "That's what we have to figure out."

"And everyone is here to do that? The police, FBI agents and Secret Service?" She didn't look entirely pleased about this. "It seems overly complicated."

"It's bureaucracy. It's rarely simple, but it also means more hands on deck to unpack this mystery."

"Okay." She sighed. "But no more metaphors. Puzzles and ship decks? I can hardly keep up." The corners of her mouth curled.

Jude had the sudden urge to hug her. Maybe even press his lips to hers—if Tyler wasn't looking. He didn't know where on earth the sensation came from, but he couldn't dwell on it now. There was no time to unpack his feelings for her.

There were too many unanswered questions. He was working, and it was crossing a line to get involved with a potential witness every-one—except him—also considered a possible accessory. Things would be different when he figured out what the missing link was.

"You're safe here. You don't have to worry."

She nodded. "It just feels weird to suddenly not have to look over my shoulder."

He rubbed between her shoulder blades, just to reinforce the reassurance. Zoe leaned into his side and gave him a smile. When she pulled away, she said, "Thank you. I don't know why, but that made me feel better."

"Me, too." He didn't know why, either. Her comfort level didn't affect him, aside from the fact that he was doing his job if she relaxed. Maybe she'd become so important to him in so short of a time that he needed her to feel safe around him. Jude had never felt like this before; it was hard to process it when it was all so new.

He got them all signed in, and walked them to the conference room Agent Daniels had assigned them. Agent Fronter was there, sipping from a full mug of coffee. The line of his body was taut as he stared out the window. Jude wondered what he was bracing for.

"Hey."

His colleague turned. "Jude." He strode over

and stuck his hand out. They shook, and he moved his hand toward Zoe.

"This is Zoe, and her son, Tyler, who you've met already."

"Steve Fronter. Nice to meet you two officially." He shook both of their hands, then turned to Jude. "Can I talk to you briefly?"

Jude nodded and asked Zoe, "You'll be okay in here for a minute?"

Only when she answered "Yes" did he step back out into the hall with Steve.

As soon as Jude stepped out of Zoe's earshot, his colleague said, "She's a looker."

"Really?" Jude folded his arms.

Steve lifted both hands. "Fine. I haven't noticed. No one noticed, in fact."

"Did you call me out here for that, or for something actually important?"

"Fine." Steve shrugged one shoulder. "I'm just saying, you should go for it. You've been single for a while—"

Jude cut him off. "She's only here to give her statement, and then she's leaving."

"So convince her to stay," Steve said. "Let the team take care of her. We can get her in protective custody and make sure she and the kid are okay."

"His name is Tyler."

"I just think you should go for it. We've

all seen what happens when one of us lets a woman get away."

Milsner had been a bear ever since his wife left.

"I'll figure it out," Jude said. "And I don't need your help." He was trying to keep a distance from Zoe, especially if she was just going to leave.

His colleague, who evidently thought he was Jude's romance advisor, sighed. "Fine."

Jude said, "I'm going to see where they're at with the questioning. Keep an eye on Zoe and Tyler."

Fronter nodded. "Sure."

Jude didn't really want to leave them, not with the couple of days they'd had. Tyler especially had been traumatized. He didn't know how the kid was keeping it together as well as he was. But Jude did want to know what was happening. They'd finally brought the Laundromat killer in. Surely this was the break they needed to wrap up the case and make Zoe safe for good.

For now, she was here and they were okay. He would take her statement soon enough.

Tyler bounced in his seat. "And then Jude said, 'Tyler—'" her son made his voice comically low to mimic Jude's "'—you stay here with Agent Fronter.' And he raced off into the woods to rescue you." His words let off, but he had an expectant look on his face, like he was waiting for her to say something.

"What?"

"Did he shoot the guy, Mom? Did he?"

Her son's enthusiasm for Jude was cute and frustrating at the same time. "Tyler, he did what any police officer would have done if they'd been there." Her son didn't need to think there was anything special about the things Jude had done for them. "He made sure you were protected, and then he came to help me. He caught the bad guy, the one who hurt Aunty Ember and Andrew. That's what cops do."

"He's a Secret Service agent, Mom."

"It's a kind of cop."

"I know the difference."

"Okay." She wasn't going to argue with him. She didn't have the energy to do it, even if he thought he knew everything about Jude…and the law.

Steve set a mug of coffee in front of Zoe and a juice box in front of Tyler. "You think Jude is pretty cool, huh?"

"He's the best!"

There was *plenty* about Jude that was special. Zoe had a hard time not swooning over him the way Tyler did, but she had the restraint born of adulthood.

A mortgage, a divorce and having her life threatened had tempered whatever enthusiasm she'd once possessed. And so, while there was plenty about Jude to dwell on, she was trying not to. An attachment wouldn't help her get on with her life—once they were safe— if her heart was still tied to Jude. And now she was going to have to help Tyler discover a new hero.

She should probably point out the fact that Jude was human, just like everyone else. But she couldn't do it. Her heart couldn't speak those words, even if honesty was best.

Steve leaned across the table toward Tyler, a conspiratorial look on his face. "Want to hear my Jude story?"

Zoe felt her eyes widen. She shot the agent a look. Hopefully he would get her message to keep it appropriate. She didn't want him telling her son a battle tale about Jude that glorified violence.

Steve's gaze flickered, then he said, "Law enforcement baseball tournament. That's what it was. Your friend Jude comes up to bat and hits a home run, right out of the park." He grinned.

Tyler let the juice straw fall from his open

mouth. "He did?" When the agent nodded, her son said, "Awesome! I can't throw it very far. I like football way better."

"You should ask Jude if he'll toss a ball around with you when y'all get some free time." Steve smiled, like that was a great idea.

It was a terrible idea. Jude didn't need to play with her son. That wasn't going to help any of them keep an emotional distance from each other.

"Awesome!"

Zoe sighed. She wanted to groan aloud, but didn't think that would help. She wanted Tyler to have fun, and he certainly needed it. Was Jude really what was best for him? Sure, her son loved him now. But what about after they left?

Parenting was all about outsmarting them. Zoe didn't want to be the bad guy. Part of her wanted to explain the dilemma to Jude, get a second opinion. Have some backup when Tyler inevitably asked him to play catch.

But Jude wasn't her sounding board. He wasn't her partner in parenting her son. That job should have gone to his father, but Nathan had decided his own happiness was more important than his son's. He hadn't even seen Tyler since he'd packed his things and left.

That thought shored up her determination

to stay distant from Jude. Nathan had found her lacking. Would Jude think so, too? Zoe wondered if maybe going through that with Jude wouldn't hurt her the way it had with Nathan. There was every possibility it would destroy her.

An amazing man like him finding her unworthy? Zoe didn't ever want to go through that.

Zoe tried not to react when he walked through the door, though she could feel her face attempting to light up. Ugh. So needy. Tyler raced over and hugged his hero around the waist, getting any attention off her, which was great. Zoe looked up, her face hot despite her attempts to stop any reaction. *We're leaving soon. We'll probably never even see him again.*

Steve's gaze was on hers, knowing and entirely too pleased about it for her liking. So what if she was attracted to Jude? It didn't mean she was going to throw herself at him. Despite the fact that she wouldn't mind one of those sweet hugs he'd just given Tyler, it was way too risky.

Steve quit his study of her and turned to Jude. "Got an update?"

"A hit on his fingerprints."

Zoe turned to him then, trying to keep her feelings to herself. "You have his prints?"

Tyler bounced back over to her and sat with his juice again.

"The agents took them when they brought him in. They're making him sweat for now, but we found out who he is." Jude paused, which made her wonder for a second who the man was. "His name is Terrence Willis."

"Tucker Wilson." She knew from what Moose had told her that it was harder to slip up on maintaining a new identity if the assumed name was close to the real name. "Who is he, really?"

Jude hesitated again. "We'll figure this out, Zoe. You don't have to worry."

"Just tell me."

"It was a really loose link, and buried so deep we almost didn't catch it. There's a sealed juvenile file and the agents are following up. But it's his family we're interested in." Jude pressed his lips together, then said, "The CEO, Alan Reskin? Terrence is his wife's second cousin."

TWELVE

Zoe pushed her chair away from the table and paced to the end of the conference room and back. Jude seemed to switch to worry for her instead of worry over what she might say or do. He said, "I'm convinced now, more than I have been so far at least, that your troubles and my investigation are connected. We just don't know exactly how."

Steve stood, as well. "What does Cousin Terrence have to do with money going in and out of the company?"

Jude said, "I think Alan Reskin is trying to cover up what he did, using the black sheep of the family to do his dirty work. I think he sent the cousin to silence Zoe and terrorize her into never telling anyone what she saw."

"But he hasn't been trying to kill me," she said. "When we were in the woods he said things had changed. And that was after a different man gave Tyler his own message. I think whatever reasoning there was caused Terrence to take things in a new direction. He intended to kill me today, instead of kidnapping me, but you showed up." She sucked in a breath. "Alan wanted things done quietly, with no fallout. What if he's the one who told Tyler to tell me to testify?"

"That would mean something had changed. Perhaps with the woman who seems to be involved." Jude frowned and glanced once at Tyler.

It helped he was so concerned about her son. It made Zoe feel all the more secure. Jude didn't have to worry about Tyler as much as he clearly did.

"But you got him." Steve clapped once. "Now we just have to find Alan, and figure out what he did."

"Find him?" Jude asked.

Steve shrugged. "I mean pick him up. Once we have the evidence on what exactly went down then we can call the district attorney."

Zoe glanced between them. "What about the cousin—isn't he being interviewed by those detectives? He'll confess to killing Moose, right?"

Jude said, "That would be good enough for the police to bring a conviction, but we need evidence, as well. We can't convict someone on a confession alone, and it's the same for the FBI. It's one of the rules we have to abide by."

"Oh." She rubbed Tyler's hair just for comfort, though he seemed perfectly happy. More like excited, really, over what was going on. "So you're going to find out who that woman was?" She didn't want to use the word *dead* but it was there nonetheless.

Jude said, "That's where I'm headed as soon as I get your statement. To the parking lot where you saw her, so I can see the scene for myself."

She was glad he said it like that as it meant there was a chance he actually believed her. Until he had evidence to prove otherwise, at least. "Do you think you'll find anything?"

"Probably not, but I want to see it."

She nodded. All the energy she'd had dissipated, and she sat.

"You'll be okay here for a little bit longer?"

"Do I have much choice?"

Jude gave her a small smile. "We're going to arrange a safe house for tonight, okay? Once we're done, it'll be late. Tomorrow you can go wherever you want."

She could just walk out of this building with her son right now. Was she going to? No. Not just because she actually did feel safe at the moment. She wanted to get as far away from this as possible but her shoulder hurt and she was exhausted. Ten hours of safe, deep sleep would be far better than a late-night trip to who knew where.

Leaving was a great idea. In principle. The execution of it was turning out to have a whole lot of issues she hadn't been ready for.

"Thank you." She included Steve in it, which made the man blink. Zoe didn't have the energy to figure out why he seemed surprised she'd be courteous.

While Steve stayed with Tyler, Zoe and Jude went over what she had seen. Then he asked her enough questions she wound up going over it all another time. Until she said, "That's it, Jude."

He frowned. The longer he stayed here staring at her with those eyes, the worse things were going to get. He was like a tractor beam of brooding. She wanted to hug him, and let him solve all of her problems. Those capable shoulders could carry her stress so much better than she was doing.

"If you're sure." He waited.

Zoe thought back to that night in the parking lot. "I'm sure I want you to find out who she was. I want to know if she's dead, and if I really saw what I thought I did."

He nodded, "Okay."

* * *

Jude strode through the parking lot, the company's head of security trailing him. He didn't pull the map from his pocket Zoe had drawn. He'd memorized where she'd been and where the man and prone woman were in relation to her. She was no artist, but neither was he, and her directions were clear enough he got the idea.

"What did you say you were looking for?"

"The Secret Service is conducting routine security tests on financial infrastructure that keep our economy safe, and I wanted to get an idea of building security as well, since I'm here." He'd filed a report with the related documents, just so this wouldn't be a total lie.

When he was almost in the right area Jude glanced around the parking lot like he was looking for cameras. Not that he expected to find them—the CEO would never be so careless as to commit a crime where it could be recorded. Or had he just known he'd be able to hide the trail…perhaps with some help?

If Alan Reskin had killed a woman down here, wouldn't this man have been brought in as part of the cleanup? Jude couldn't dismiss it as an option, so he had to not make it obvious he was basically looking for blood on the floor. Alan had taken the woman in his car, but there had to have been evidence to clean up.

He nodded, as though satisfied with what he saw, and then trailed between cars via the vicinity of where Zoe had indicated. "Have you worked here for long?"

"Fifteen years. Before that I worked private security."

"That's impressive." Jude had figured the guard was former military, but wouldn't know until later when he ran the man's identity. "Do you like working for BioWell?"

The man sniffed. "It's a job." He didn't ask Jude about being a Secret Service agent. Did he have someone in an office upstairs, running the check? Impersonating a federal agent was a serious crime, but too many people were dumbstruck by a shiny badge and forgot to ask basic questions.

Even Zoe had taken his word for it.

Which brought his thoughts back to her. Again. Jude shook his head, as though that would stop his brain from going back there. It seemed all his mind wanted to do was think about her. Muse over her. Wonder about them together. Did they have a future? Could he really help her?

Jude took a breath and prayed each of those questions, casting each burden onto his Lord.

He might fail, but God would not. Jude was content to trust in His help.

"Is there any way I can see your security office? I'd like to get a look at your sctup."

The man sniffed again. "Sure."

Which meant he wasn't threatened by Jude's observing. When the man walked him to the elevator, the pace was faster than Jude normally moved. Which made him wonder if this guy needed to prove he was better. Was it a power play, making him uncomfortable by walking so fast? He said nothing in the elevator, which was fine with Jude. He got the opportunity to study the man. But he gave nothing away.

"Any idca where Alan Reskin is?" Jude asked. "I'd like to speak with him, if that's possible."

"He's on vacation right now. A cabin in the middle of nowhere. No cell signal, no internet. No contact. He'll be back in a few days, though."

It was a specific answer, but also vague. And did not include an offer to get Jude in contact with the man when he returned. "I'll have to make an appointment with his secretary, then."

"She's on vacation, as well."

"At the same time?"

"Makes sense if you ask me," the man said. "Nothing to do while he isn't here."

Jude didn't point out the fact that that was basically ridiculous, but he wanted to. Alan might very well have been in town that morning, being as Zoe thought it was this man who'd delivered his "message" to Tyler. The head of his security probably didn't want Jude to expose his lie. Or his ignorance. Jude was content to keep the knowledge to himself for now. If Alan really was covering up a murder, Jude couldn't give away anything that might warn him to go into hiding before they found him.

The only way they could prove someone had died here would be to bring a black light and some Luminol that would show blood even if it had been cleaned away. With no body it would be hard to prove a murder had occurred. Unless he found a considerable amount of blood residue. Otherwise it could have simply been a fight, or an accident.

Zoe grew more restless the longer Jude was gone. Tyler was handling it worse than she was, which gave her something to focus on. She'd rather not have spent the hour telling him to calm down, or to sit still, though. Not that she truly blamed him for being restless.

The boy was…well, he was *a boy*. He needed a park to run around in. Instead of being cooped up here where both of them were going crazy.

"Should I get him a snack or something?"

She considered the agent's words. "Sugar probably isn't a good idea."

Steve Fronter had been replaced by a female agent shortly after Jude left. She was nice enough, though maybe she didn't know much about little boys. Zoe didn't hold it against her.

The agent nodded. "I could see how that might be true. I'm sure we can find something in the vending machine. Maybe some nuts."

Tyler perked up. "I love nuts."

She stood. "What do you say, little man? Want to go with me and find something to munch on?"

Zoe's stomach growled. A snack was probably a good idea for both of them.

Tyler jumped up. "Yeah!"

"Grab me something, too, okay?"

He nodded and raced out with the agent.

Zoe felt bad about it, but she breathed a sigh of relief when he left the room. Her arm was starting to get sore again and it wasn't time to take more pain meds yet.

Zoe laid her head back on the cushy chair, thankful the government had sprung for nice tall-backed office chairs for their agents to sit in while they were conferencing. She smiled to herself, then shut her eyes.

All she saw was Jude.

Then the woman, lying on the ground with Alan Reskin standing over her. A shiver moved through her. He had always seemed like a nice enough man—or so she'd thought. She'd worked in his company but had never met him. All she knew was that he was powerful and wealthy.

He was said to be happily married. Nothing to indicate murderous tendencies. Beyond that she didn't know much, and wouldn't have had the chance to, either. Her job was to stare at columns of numbers all day, not schmooze with people who wouldn't look twice at a single mom who only needed to work so she didn't get evicted. They were worlds apart.

Or they had been, until that night.

Zoe shuddered, which shot more pain through her shoulder. A tear rolled down her cheek. Where was Jude? What was taking so long? Surely he'd found where the woman had died. Maybe it was impossible, but what would she do otherwise? Zoe would look like she'd lied. Though how had she made up Terrence Willis trying to kill her, or those people hurting Andrew?

"Zoe?"

She opened her eyes and saw Steve in the hall. "Is Tyler okay?" He was probably terrorizing the agents in the office. They'd dealt with worse threats than a seven-year-old boy, so surely they were able to handle it.

"You should come with me."

Not liking his look, Zoe got up. Her head swam from pain and lack of food. She braced a hand on the table before she got her bearings enough to walk to him. He didn't help her. Zoe walked with him down the hall. "Is Tyler being a nuisance? I should have told him to behave himself with that agent."

"I'm sure he's fine. This is about something else."

Was it Jude? Maybe something had happened to him. "What is it?"

His lips thinned, but he said nothing. Steve led her through an exit door...to a stairwell? Zoe stepped through and then turned.

She didn't get all the way around before his arms wrapped around her from behind. His grip squeezed her injured shoulder and she cried out. Before the sound could travel beyond the two of them, he clapped a hand over her mouth.

"Don't scream and your son will live."

THIRTEEN

Jude listened to the phone ring in his car as he drove back to the office, but Steve didn't pick up. He called Agent Milsner next.

When the agent answered, he said, "Any update on finding the CEO?" Jude hardly believed Reskin was on vacation.

"Not yet," Milsner said. "Anything from his office besides that security video?"

"Not a thing. We'd need crime scene techs if we want to dig below the surface." There was a chance that trace evidence had been left behind even if the scene was cleaned extensively. If a woman had died in that parking lot, then there was every chance they'd find proof. But only if they were able to get a warrant for an extensive search.

"You think she really saw a murder?"

Jude's stomach clenched. He wanted to defend her, but wasn't about to get angry at his colleague for asking a logical question. "I think we need to dig more. Find Alan Reskin and ask a whole lot of questions." It would help if Zoe could identify the woman, as well. Until they knew who she was they wouldn't know why she might've been killed.

Jude had no idea how they would figure out who the woman was, short of Zoe looking at thousands of photos. Talk about a needle in a haystack.

"Parks and Tanner went to Reskin's house."

"Good," Jude said. "Between the cousin we have in custody, the woman who set the fire and Alan Reskin, all we have is a trifecta of something and not the first clue what it is."

"Or precisely how it relates to the investigation."

"True." Jude flipped on his blinker and turned onto the street where the Secret Service office was located. "Later."

Jude hung up the call and headed inside the building. Passing through security took a whole lot less time without having to sign Zoe and Tyler in, and within minutes he was in the elevator headed upstairs.

His thoughts stayed on Zoe, and the danger she would face if she ran—all on her own without anyone to look out for her. He didn't want to consider her getting hurt but he couldn't go. He wanted her close, and it didn't have anything at all to do with the investigation. Instead it had everything to do with the way she'd looked up at him from the floor of the Laundromat. And every glance since then.

If Zoe could've identified the woman it would have helped. With nothing to narrow down her identity other than the fact that she'd been blond, that would be nearly impossible. Zoe's statement had included the fact that she hadn't seen the woman's face.

They could start with staff at BioWell, if the company consented to release names of all their employees. If they pushed for a warrant, Jude figured the Secret Service wouldn't have enough to get one. But who knew if the dead woman even worked there?

He prayed the conversation between the agents and Terrence Willis yielded a result, as well as the search for Alan Reskin. They needed something that would allow them to put the criminals behind bars, or Zoe and Tyler would never be safe.

He checked the conference room, but didn't see Zoe or Tyler, then went to the closest manned desk and asked the agent, "Have you seen the woman who was in there?" When the man shook his head, Jude said, "What about Agent Fronter?" Maybe Steve had taken her somewhere, so she could walk instead of sitting for hours.

"Haven't seen him in a while."

"And Terrence Willis?"

"The detectives took him back to their station to get booked in."

"Thanks." He'd need to find out what the man had said, but right now he needed to figure out where Zoe and her son had gone. Jude turned with a sigh, and surveyed the office. Cubicles and a government-issue printer with an out-of-order sign taped to it. Where were they?

Tyler rounded the corner at the end of the office, emerging from the hall where the vending machines were. The kid had chocolate all around his mouth. He grinned, clutching a packet of trail mix and two juice boxes.

Jude waited until the kid caught up to him. The last few steps Tyler picked up his pace until he collided with Jude, who hugged the kid back but was careful he didn't get food smears on his shirt. "Hey. Any idea where your mom is?" He glanced at the female agent who had escorted the boy, including her in his question.

Tyler said, "No," while the female agent frowned and strode to the conference room.

"She isn't in here."

"I know," Jude said. "That's why I asked. So where did she go?"

"Good question."

Even Tyler looked worried now.

"Don't worry, we'll find her."

Zoe lost her footing on the concrete steps of the stairwell and stumbled. Steve's punishing grip on her arms never loosened. He'd secured his tie around her mouth and it cut into her cheeks. She could barely breathe. Even though her nose wasn't blocked it still felt like she couldn't draw in air. Her shoulder was screaming, the pain so bad she'd nearly blacked out a couple of times.

"Nice try," the agent said. "But falling isn't going to help you."

She said nothing. The words would have been garbled behind the gag anyway. She found her footing on the next landing, but he didn't slow. He just kept dragging her down and down and down. What would he do when he got her to his car? And how could he get her past the office security?

Would this agent kill her himself or was he taking her to her former boss for him to kill her? The crazy cousin was in jail, so he couldn't hurt her anymore. And yet there was still so much danger.

God, help me.

The words were foreign, but she needed aid. God could send help. She didn't know much about how to be His follower, but she knew He helped people who stayed close to Him. Like Jude.

Please.

Her breath came in gasps, and black spots pricked in the edges of her vision. Her stomach roiled but now was not the time to be sick. She had to get out of this man's grasp, but attempting to kick him and fight him hadn't gotten her anywhere. He'd slammed her against the wall. The door handle on that floor had dug into her side. She would have a huge bruise there tomorrow.

No, fighting wouldn't help. But if she passed out then he would have to carry her, wouldn't he? Zoe swayed more than was necessary on the next set of stairs. She closed her eyes slowly, like she was losing consciousness, and prayed he would buy her act. That she could slow him down long enough for someone to realize she was missing and be able to find her. Was Jude even back in the office yet?

Steven shifted her in his arms. Zoe took the opportunity and went limp. With a grunted curse, the man shifted and then his shoulder was in her stomach. All the air escaped her as he hefted her up. Her arm dangled and she wanted to scream at the pain that shocked through her shoulder.

He shifted her. Just a short bounce, and his bone prodded a different part of her stomach. Then he started walking. Zoe moaned; she couldn't help it. His grip made her hips hurt as well, and every step down jarred her even more. Zoe had to resist the urge to revisit with her breakfast, even while the temptation to pass out increased.

But what could she do to stop him if she was out cold?

He rounded the landing. Zoe caught a glimpse of the floor number. Three. On the next set of stairs down she hooked her foot on the handrail and managed to drag him back for a second. That earned her a sharp slap on the back of her leg, which startled her enough to make her lose her grip.

"I should just shoot you right now for that."

He kept going until he reached the underground parking lot. Steve stopped, and everything in Zoe stilled. He was going to get away with this—get away with *her*. He took a breath and pushed open the door.

The air in the parking lot was cooler—a basement encased in concrete—and smelled like motor oil. It brought back all the memories she had of that night. Alan Reskin.

A man who ran a pharmaceutical company should care about people's health. But no, he'd hurt a woman. Zoe thought back to the woman's form until the mental image dissipated. She'd looked familiar, but where did she know the woman from? Maybe she worked at the company. Perhaps the man had been having an affair with a colleague, or it had to do with the case Jude was working on. Money or passion—those were top reasons for murder, right?

Later on, when she got out of this latest predicament—*if* she got out of it—she would have to figure out who the woman had been.

Steven grunted and stopped.

Then she heard Jude's voice. "Put her down, Steve."

"Move, Brauer. Let me pass and I won't kill her, but you have to let me go." The desperation in his voice wasn't something Zoe had expected. He didn't want to do this?

"Put her down and explain what's going on." She could hear the tightness of Jude's jaw muscles in the tone of his voice. She didn't want him to have to shoot his friend, but knew he would if the man refused to let her go.

"Steve," Jude barked. "Put. Her. Down."

* * *

Jude stared down a man he'd considered a friend. How could he attempt to abduct Zoe, and from the Secret Service office of all places? He couldn't understand any of this.

Steve took a step to the side.

Jude matched it. "This isn't going anywhere. You're done, Fronter. You've pushed too far, but you're not getting any farther. And definitely not with Zoe. Now put her down. I'm not going to ask again. I'm just going to shoot you."

He hoped it didn't come to a shootout. There was too much risk of Zoe getting seriously hurt. But if it came to that, he was ready. A good half a dozen agents were now peppered around the garage, hidden behind pillars and cars. Their SWAT guys had been called in.

Jude didn't want this to dissolve into a firefight. "Steve." He barked the man's name like it was an order.

"Okay." Fronter's face flushed, and he lowered Zoe to the ground.

Jude couldn't stare at her; he had to keep his attention on Steve. But he wanted to. Was she alive? Unconscious? How badly was she hurt? While he wanted her to move, he also prayed she would stay put. He didn't need her being more of a pawn in this than she already was. Zoe deserved better than to be treated as a bargaining chip for anyone who needed to get in the good graces of the person pulling strings here. He didn't think that person was Steve Fronter.

"Now pull your gun. Slowly. Drop it to the ground, Fronter." He didn't need the man armed when they had this conversation.

Steve did as he asked, his face now contorted. But not in anger. It looked more like sadness, or desperation.

"What's going on?"

When Fronter said nothing, Jude asked, "Why are you abducting my witness?" He could have called her something else, but this needed to be impersonal. Steve already knew Jude's heart was involved. Neither one of them needed reminding of that fact.

Steve looked up at the concrete ceiling, like he was studying the ridges of the design. "I had to do it."

Jude waited.

"They said they'd hurt my family. It won't pay off what I owe, but they'll cancel part of my debt. I had to bring Zoe to them."

"Why does Reskin want her?"

Steve shook his head. "How should I know? He just said bring her."

"How does he know about your debt?"

"I don't know," he yelled. "It's all online. I guess he found out I've been gambling, and he leveraged it. He threatened my family."

Jude winced at the desperation in his voice. "I'm sorry."

"I *had* to do this."

No, he didn't. But Jude thought pointing that out right now might not be helpful. The agency could have helped him, but at the least they should have known this leverage over one of their agents was a risk. One they couldn't afford.

The agents behind Fronter had closed in.

"What does he want with her?" He'd asked it already, but Steve might give him something now.

The man sighed. "I don't know. I can guess."

"Was he going to kill her?"

"You think I'd have risked my career just for a chat? He said he'd tell Agent Daniels and my family about my debts. I'd have been ruined. My wife would leave me and I'd be out of a job."

"And that was worth Zoe's life to you?"

"I'm not noble like you, Jude. I'm not an all holier than thou, church guy. You pray about everything, and I just have to do my best. Okay? That's all." His gaze turned hard. Unrepentant about the fact that he'd put Zoe in danger and done it to save his own skin.

The agents grabbed him, wasting no time with the cuffs. They walked Steve Fronter away, and Jude raced to Zoe. He crouched by her and saw that her eyes were open.

"Ouch."

Jude shut his eyes and touched his forehead to hers. "Zoe." She was all right. The relief that moved through him swept the thoughts from his mind.

"Tyler?" The question was soft.

Jude leaned back so he could see her eyes. "He's fine."

She smiled. Lifted her chin.

Jude touched his lips to hers for a brief moment and found there a promise that he held to himself. But now wasn't the time for this. He leaned back and placed another kiss on her forehead, then gathered her into his arms and carried her to the elevator. Zoe's grip on him was light, but the softness felt good. When he emerged on the right floor the office was in a frenzy. He dropped Zoe in the conference room with Tyler, glanced once into her eyes to assure himself that she was fine and then stepped out.

He asked the closest agent, "What's going on?" All this commotion wasn't over Steve

Fronter's actions, was it? They were likely riled up by one of their own turning this way, but he couldn't help thinking this might be more.

"The two detectives were ambushed on the way to the police station. Terrence Willis was set free. He's in the wind."

FOURTEEN

Zoe waited until Jude rounded the car before she opened the door and stepped out, as he'd instructed. The house was huge, bigger than anywhere she'd ever lived before. "This is the safe house?"

Jude nodded. He didn't look at her, though. His eyes scanned the dark street around them. Could he see something she didn't?

She bit her lip. "Everything okay?"

"Yes." The word was clipped. "Let's get inside, where it's safe."

Tyler held her hand tight in his. She couldn't decide if her son was freaked out or just tired. Probably a combination of both, considering. The pain in her shoulder had lessened thanks to the medication she'd taken. All that jarring meant it would hurt more, and for longer, but thankfully she hadn't pulled her stitches out or she'd have had to revisit the doctor.

She was supposed to be leaving town, but

now the man who wanted to kill her was loose again. She was locked in indecision, unsure whether to stay or go.

Inside the house was cool and sparse, all gray floor tiles and white walls. "It looks like a model home they spruce up extra fancy so you think your stuff will look that good when you move in," she said. "Never does, though, I'd imagine."

Jude glanced at her, but didn't smile. "We have enough bedrooms that you can both have your own, but…"

"We'll share."

"That's what I figured. One has a king bed, so there's plenty of room for you and Tyler."

She glanced at her son then. "You okay, kiddo?"

He nodded, still clinging to her hand.

"Want to see what's on TV?"

"Sure." His usual enthusiasm for screen time was muted, but he flopped down on the couch and a moment later she heard a cooking show come on. Whether it was cable or satellite wouldn't matter. Tyler was so technologically minded he figured out any complicated remote fast, whether he'd used it before or not.

The memory of him figuring out how to clear off her email inbox when she couldn't find the setting fell away and she went in search of Jude.

He stood in the marble-and-chrome kitchen, his head in a fridge bigger than she'd ever seen. Was everything in this house massive? She felt like Goldilocks, but hopefully no bears would try to eat her. Except now she'd thought that it would probably play a starring role in her nightmares tonight.

Zoe sighed and settled on one of the bar stools. The leather top creaked like it was brand new.

Jude shut the fridge and turned. "Spaghetti?"

She nodded. "Tyler would love that."

"They stocked the fridge for us, so there's plenty of food. There are also agents stationed out front and in the street behind us." He paused. "It's safe here, so you can rest."

He'd been like this, all business, since they'd gotten in the car. Zoe knew about Terrence's escape. She'd overheard two of the agents talking about it. That agent had tried to abduct her at the same time. What did it mean? Why have two concurrently running plans? What kind of person had those resources? Even someone like the CEO of a major company couldn't hide his activities for long if multiple people knew. The more who were informed, the greater the risk the secret got out.

Perilous business, if anyone was going to ask her. But they hadn't, because they were all federal agents and she wasn't.

Zoe felt like dead weight. Maybe Jude was keeping his distance because he didn't want to have to keep saving her. He'd probably rather be out hunting for Terrence instead of here babysitting her. Was he tired of her? Zoe sucked in a breath and looked at the marble countertop. What if he didn't want to be around her anymore? He probably thought she needed to learn some self-defense skills or something.

"Spaghetti would be great, but you don't have to make it. You don't even have to stay, if you don't want to."

"What?" It wasn't exactly harsh, but his tone wasn't superfriendly, either.

"Oh," she said. "Well, I mean...don't feel like you *need* to stay here with us." She glanced around and realized that with the open plan she could see the living room. Tyler's head wasn't visible above the couch, but he always lay down when he watched TV anyway. A cartoon was playing on the screen.

When she looked back, Jude was frowning.

Zoe continued, "I'm sure there's an agent who could stay with us if you want to do something else." The idea of leaving her protection to someone who wasn't Jude made her stomach churn, but she could do it. Most law officers were good people trying to do a good job.

She would rather Jude stayed here, but if he wanted to go how could she stop him?

He opened his mouth to answer, and his phone rang. Still frowning, he answered it. Why did he look mad anyway? She was trying to give him an out. Wasn't that a good thing?

"Mom," he said, his face immediately softening. "How is Dad?" He listened for a minute. "Good. I'm glad." Pause. "You do? Oh, okay." He held the phone out to Zoe. "She wants to talk to you."

Zoe took the phone. "Leanne?"

"Hello, my dear. How are you holding up? The police officers who arrived here told us what happened."

"I'm fine now. Jude made sure the agent couldn't take me anywhere." He had saved her. That was why she figured he was sick of doing it by now. "We're at a safe house—"

Jude's head whipped around from chopping an onion. "Don't tell her where it is."

She shot him a look. As if she would, but didn't he even trust his own mother? She said to Leanne, "How is Andrew?"

"Sitting up, eating pudding and driving the nurses crazy." Leanne chuckled.

"And Ember?" When she'd called the hospital from the Secret Service office, Ember had mentioned Leanne's visit. She wanted to see her sister for herself, but this was the next best thing. And safer for everyone.

"I walked with one of the officers—they're staying with us—over to see your sister. They moved her next door, and she has protection, as well—"

Had Jude set that up because of what happened to her?

"She's getting some color back already."

"Thank you so much, Leanne," Zoe said. "It's really great to hear. Not that you all need police protection, though I'm glad you have it. But I'm happy to hear the patients are doing better."

"Me, too. Now, you stay safe, and give that little boy of yours a hug from me."

"I will."

She hung up, and Zoe set the phone on the counter. She hopped off the stool and went to look at Tyler. His eyes were closed, and his little-boy chest rose and fell with each slow breath.

She ran her hand through his hair, thankful to God that he was okay. God had sent Jude to save her from Steve Fronter. Believing in God's power, and His love, was easier now.

Easiest of all was sending up a small prayer for God to watch over her son.

Zoe wandered back to the kitchen, wanting to ask Jude about his relationship with God. That scowl was back on his face. Sure, he was cooking, but he probably wanted to be anywhere else. Maybe he even wanted to go be with his father at the hospital.

"Jude." Zoe cleared her throat. "Um, someone else can stay with us if you want to go."

"You mentioned that already." He sounded mad.

"Okay, so?" What was his answer going to be?

"So do you want milk or water with dinner?"

Jude nearly threw the spoon at the wall. After everything he'd done for her, Zoe wanted him to go? He could hardly believe that after he'd saved her again and again, she just wanted any old agent to take care of her and her son.

The fact that he was about to make dinner for them, and that they'd eat it together—like a family—had just hit him. Then Zoe had told him to leave.

"Water." The uncertainty in her tone bothered him, but he pushed it aside.

Clearly they were on different pages here.

"And Tyler?"

"He's asleep. Can we leave him a plate?"

Jude nodded but didn't turn. He got three plates from the cupboard and served the simple meal.

"So, you cook."

"Only a few things. But a bachelor has to be able to feed himself or I'd be huge, eating fast food all the time. Or spending way too much money eating out good meals every day." He saw her nod out of the corner of his eye. "Instead, I'm saving to get a house. I almost have enough for a down payment."

"That's impressive," she said, though there was a note of caution in her voice. "Most people live paycheck to paycheck, and never have enough to put down on a house."

Jude shrugged. "I know what I want out of life. A home, a family. A career I enjoy that gives me the opportunity to make a difference."

"That's a good dream."

He handed her plate across the breakfast bar, and then took his and sat on the stool beside her. Didn't she have dreams for what the future would be like? He could see her in a big yard, watching Tyler play with a dog. Something cool, like a husky.

"Can I borrow your phone for a second?"

He pulled it out, but before handing it over, asked, "You need to call someone?"

Zoe shook her head. "The company put pictures from the picnic we had last summer on social media. I wanted to look at them and see if any of the staff looks like the woman I saw in the parking lot." She flushed. "I can't believe I didn't think of doing that earlier."

Jude unlocked the phone and slid it over. "Don't worry about that. You've been under a lot of stress. It's good you thought of it now." And he really meant it. She was helping them out, though most of her motivation was because she was getting herself in danger at almost every turn. The constant attacks were providing him and his colleagues with leads, even if she didn't plan it like that. Jude just prayed they would get more usable intel from Steve Fronter.

Zoe scrolled through images on the phone screen. "Nothing," she said. "There are blonde women, but none of them look like the one I saw."

He looked at the screen, at the last picture she'd studied. "Reskin was at the party?"

She nodded. "I never talked to him. He probably didn't even notice me. I haven't worked there long, so it's not like we socialize." She stared at the phone, and absently continued to scroll through pictures.

"I guess."

"I just wish I knew who the woman—" Zoe gasped.

"What is it?"

Her face turned white and she put her hand over her mouth. Jude slid the phone so he could see it. The picture on screen was of Alan Reskin and a woman. The woman was a blonde, and Jude knew exactly who she was. He said gently, "Is this the woman you saw in the parking lot that night?"

Zoe sucked in a breath, her meal forgotten. His was going cold, as well. He wasn't even all that hungry. "That woman…" She took another breath. "Yes, that's her." Zoe lifted the phone, turned it sideways and tilted the screen. She'd seen the woman lying down. Was she making sure?

She nodded. "I'm pretty sure it's her."

Jude bit down on his molars. "Zoe."

She turned to him, a frown marring the soft skin above her brows. "What?"

"That's Mrs. Reskin."

"It is?" She looked at the picture. "I knew she seemed familiar. Is she…missing?"

"I don't know." Jude shrugged. "I can ask around, but I'd think if the man's wife suddenly went missing he would probably report it to the police. We've been investigating his business. We'd have heard about it."

"That's what I would do. Unless I was involved. Although, in that case I think I'd report it just to make it look like I was innocent. Isn't that what they always do on TV, because the spouse is always the first suspect?"

Jude nodded. "The police would look into everyone close to the victim. A spouse doesn't get a free pass, even if they do seem really upset about the death or disappearance."

"That much lying makes me want to be sick. The deception…" She shook her head. "You'd have to be a really cold person to connive all that just to get away with murder."

Jude grabbed his phone and got up. "I should call this in. The agents visiting Reskin's house can find out if his wife is missing, or if she's conveniently out of town."

Assuming they were going to take Zoe's word for it with no evidence. If only there was a body this would all be so different. They were going to take Zoe's statement seriously— even an allegation of murder was too serious to brush off. But she was also making it so they would effectively accuse a man of murder with nothing to back up their assertion. If they weren't able to find proof then Alan could make all of their lives extremely difficult over this if he wanted to.

Zoe stared at him, wide-eyed. Jude said, "Try to eat something. You'll sleep better."

Not that he thought any of them would sleep at all tonight. Except Tyler, given how quiet it was in the living room.

A second later, Tyler sat up, crying out. Tears rolled down his face as he looked around the room. Zoe raced over and gathered up her son in her arms. "Mom," he cried, "the man was here. He was in the safe house."

"No one is here, honey. It's just you, me and Jude. Everything is okay."

Jude had explained what the concept of a safe house was, but apparently the kid's fears had bypassed even those assurances.

Zoe looked at him. Those wide eyes, so full of fear and helplessness. Jude said, "I'll check with the agents outside, make sure no one is skulking around. Okay?"

She nodded, and Tyler looked up from where his face had been buried in her hair.

"I'll be right back."

He headed into the hall and made the call to the car out front. It rang and rang.

No one picked up.

FIFTEEN

"They aren't answering."

She didn't like the look on Jude's face at all. Zoe shifted her son and set him on his feet, but kept him close to her side. He didn't need to know how scared she was. If she held him in a death grip he would figure out she wasn't nearly as self-assured as she felt.

"Should we go out there and check on them?" she asked. "Or call the police?" Jude's silence said more than any words ever could have. "Or should we hide?"

He held up a hand. "One second."

Zoe forced her feet to stay planted when what she wanted was to race for the door. Her instinct to flee had kicked in.

Jude dialed on his phone again, then held it to his ear. "Yeah, it's Brauer." He lowered the phone and touched a button.

The voice came through loud and clear.

"...glad you called," a man said. "Is everything okay?"

"We aren't sure. Zoe and Tyler are with me, and the agents out front aren't responding. We need backup but I have no idea what they'll be walking into."

The man yelled something she couldn't make out, then said, "Help is on the way."

"Thank you." Jude sounded genuinely grateful. "I really appreciate it."

"You're one of us, Brauer, and we take care of our own."

Zoe wondered why the man said that, considering what Steve Fronter had done. Were they all a little more wary now? Maybe this man, whoever he was, felt guilty he hadn't stopped Fronter from selling out to blackmailers. Not that he cared about her, or the fact that she'd been hurt. It was probably their pride as a federal agency that had been dinged.

"In the meantime," the man said, "you all sit tight. Maybe make use of the panic room if you think it's necessary."

"Panic room?" The question escaped before she realized it. Beside her, Tyler echoed the question.

Jude just nodded, then said, "We will," to the man on the phone. He waved them over to him and began making his way through the house.

Halfway along the hall, carpeted stairs led down below the ground floor. The basement was probably as nice as the main level, but they didn't go down there. Jude took them to a rear bedroom with a four-poster bed covered in what looked like seriously expensive blush-peach covers. Even the pillowcases had pearl embellishments.

"Seriously?" Zoe would probably never sleep in a bed like that in her entire life.

Jude glanced over. "We seized the house from a drug distributor. His wife had way too much time and money. She dolled the place up." He grinned. "The master bathroom is a sight to behold."

The man on the phone said, "We got back the file for Terrence Willis."

"Any intel helps."

Zoe frowned at Jude's comment. "Unless he's already here." She muttered the words under her breath, but he shot her a look like he'd heard and didn't appreciate her comment.

Tyler still clung to her, so she rubbed her hand between his shoulder blades. He seemed like he was doing better than she was, but he considered Jude to be his hero. Why wouldn't he be secure here with the man himself?

Jude said, "What do you have?"

"Willis got into some trouble as a teen, landed himself in juvenile detention."

"So it's a sealed record?"

"Daniels called the county sheriff in the town where he lived and got the basics. Fireworks in city limits, setting fires in trash cans. Blew up the chem lab at his school and finally set fire to a warehouse. He killed a janitor who was working there in the middle of the night."

Zoe felt her eyes widen. The man after her liked to set fires? She hadn't thought he'd set the fire at her house that had hurt Ember, but this made it sound like it was the kind of thing he did. Ember had claimed it was a woman, and now they found out Ruskin's wife's second cousin was a firebug? Had they been working together, then and now?

How was that even possible when she'd seen the woman…

Dead?

Zoe didn't even know anymore.

"The sheriff indicated an escalation. Terrence figured out what he was doing, and the fires got more sophisticated. The warehouse was rigged up. All the doors and windows secured so the guy died trying to get out. And it was a slow burn. It took hours to engulf."

Did that mean Terrence had time to set the fire at her house, kill Moose and then return to the house?

Jude turned to her, his own eyes as wide as hers probably were. "Thanks for the information. Can you let the fire department know we might need them? I don't know what's going on, but we're headed into the panic room now."

"Make contact when you can."

"Will do." Jude hung up the call. He must have seen the question in her gaze, because he said, "There's no signal in there. Just a landline that isn't connected to the rest of the house."

"He could cut it, couldn't he, if he wanted to?"

"It would be nearly impossible to figure out which wire it is, even if he's a telephone engineer—and there doesn't seem to be any evidence he has those skills. But I'm not discounting anything."

"Oh." She was just going to have to take his word for it, then. "So Terrence Willis likes fire?" Why she needed to ask this, she didn't know. Was it just nervous conversation? She didn't want to be that helpless, afraid woman, but life was life and she had to face reality.

She couldn't save herself, but maybe that was why God had sent her help.

Jude nodded, not happy. "He's a regular firebug."

"Is he going to set this house on fire?"

Tyler's question came out of nowhere. Zoe whirled to face him and crouched, so she could look in his face. "Everything is going to be okay. Jude is here, and so am I." Was he remembering when he and Ember had hidden in the bathtub? She didn't want him to relive that event, but if he did it was understandable.

Jude ran his fingers along the chair rail that cut the wall in half horizontally. He stilled on one part, and then pushed in. A door popped out. It reached the ceiling and had been completely disguised in the wall. Inside there was a couch and she could see multiple screens.

"Surveillance cameras." He glanced at Tyler. "And a fridge. Which makes it the perfect place to hide out."

He motioned them inside, and they moved into the space, which was about six by ten. Not a large room, but plenty big enough to hide in until rescue came. The Secret Service certainly knew what they were doing when they put witnesses up in a safe house.

"Do you really think he's here?"

"We aren't going to risk it."

She nodded, then realized Jude hadn't come in. "What are you—"

He started to slide the door closed. "Don't come out. No matter what you see, or hear, wait for help to come. The Secret Service knows how to get in, and they're the only ones who have the authorization to let you out."

Like that was supposed to make her feel better? One of them had tried to kidnap her. And yeah, the others probably felt really bad about it, but was she really supposed to trust them now?

"Jude—"

A man came into view right behind him. He lifted a gun high and brought it down on the back of Jude's head.

Zoe screamed. Tyler yelled. Jude fell to the ground in a slump, eyes closed. Unconscious. Was he dead?

She didn't look at the man now standing in the door—the man who had found them. She couldn't look at him or all the fear in the back of her mind would overtake her the way Tyler's was now doing. Her son was hysterical, but all Zoe could do was stare at Jude's unconscious form.

There. His chest moved.

He was breathing. *God, help us.*

Terrence lifted the gun and pointed it...at Tyler. "Shut him up or I'll do it."

Zoe gathered her son to her. It didn't do much to quiet him, but she prayed it was enough that Terrence would be satisfied and not shoot him. "What do you want with us?"

He grinned, an awful evil grin. "Now it's time for all of us to go up in flames."

Jude groaned. The pain in the back of his head was overwhelming, but he was alive so it likely wasn't more than a hard hit to his skull. He touched his hair and then blinked at his fingers. Red. Wet. That wasn't good. And where was Zoe?

The last thing he remembered was getting them in the panic room, elated that they would be safe and he could go take care of whatever problem they were in by himself.

Now they were gone.

Jude lifted his head, then sat up. His vision was blurry, and he wanted to be sick but pushed the feeling aside and felt for his weapon. Gone. He was in the doorway of the panic room and it was empty.

He didn't let the fear take hold. Just as he'd done with the nausea he ignored it and concerned himself with finding his feet. He had to get to them. If Terrence had Zoe and Tyler then Jude needed to reach them fast before the worst happened. What would he do if they were hurt…or killed? He didn't think he would be able to carry on if he lost them after all this. And even though Zoe had tried to push him away, and get another protector, he wouldn't have left her for anything.

Jude wanted to be the one to take care of her. Maybe even forever. What did his career matter when he could see himself being so happy with a family? Having that closeness, that intimacy, with her, and being a father to Tyler. What could be more important?

He stumbled through the bedroom looking for his missing weapon and the two people he cared about most. Maybe Zoe wouldn't want him permanently in her life. Maybe she wouldn't want the reminder of a time she'd been so scared. But he needed to find out what her answer would be.

He needed to ask at least the first question. Did she care about him the way he cared about her?

The doorway loomed, and he put one hand on the frame. Everything spun. He probably had a serious concussion, but considering Zoe's and Tyler's lives could be in danger it didn't rate high in importance.

Smoke filled the hallway. Jude coughed

through it, but didn't let it slow him down. He checked all the rooms and then made his way to the patio door. It slid open two inches, and then got stuck. When Jude felt through the gap, he found the thin plastic of zip ties. Trapped.

Where was the team?

He spun around and made his way through the dining room. The house was a maze of corners, rooms with two exits that connected them to the next space. It was great to hide in. Or run from someone and find available cover. But that meant it took him longer to find them.

When he did, they were huddled together on the couch. The smoke was thicker now, and Terrence paced the area between the coffee table and the hearth. Jude didn't look at Zoe and Tyler or he'd be too affected by their fear to hold his own in check. He would not let this man hurt them, but Terrence didn't seem to be trying to kill them with that gun of his—or Jude's. He held one in each hand. No, Terrence seemed to be waiting for something.

Slow burn.

Jude sneaked back to the kitchen and found a knife. He cut the ties on the patio door, and then eased it open as quietly as he could.

He did the same to the door that led to the garage but couldn't get to the front door without Terrence seeing. When he made his way back toward the dining room, he saw FBI SWAT creeping through.

The first man pulled his spare sidearm and held it out to Jude.

He whispered, "Thanks." After he'd checked the weapon, Jude used hand signals to explain where Terrence and his captives were.

The man nodded. He motioned to his guys, and they led the way since they had vests on. Jude didn't hang back too much, though.

"Hands up!"

"Freeze!"

Zoe screamed and Jude raced into the living room in time to see one SWAT guy knock the only remaining weapon from Terrence's grasp. Jude placed himself between the man and Zoe, holding Tyler behind him. When SWAT had Terrence on the ground he said, "Is a fire team working on the blaze?"

The FBI agent who'd led the team nodded. He keyed his radio. "Clear."

A siren sounded for two seconds, and then went silent. Jude figured that meant, "Copy that."

The windows were hit by a torrent of water spray, and he turned to Zoe. "Let's get out of here, okay?" She nodded and he led them both out the front door ahead of Terrence, while

Tyler clung to both of their hands. He didn't even want them to have to look at the man again. "Are either of you hurt?"

She shook her head.

"Good." He headed to the waiting ambulance anyway. His head hurt in a way that it blurred his vision and made him want to swoon. Not a good look for a hero.

He nodded to the EMT and then sat on the edge of the ambulance where the back doors were open.

When he climbed inside the ambulance, Zoe gasped. Even Tyler looked a little green.

"Head wounds always look worse than they really are." Was he attempting to reassure them, or himself?

Before she could respond, a police officer said, "Ma'am, can I ask you some questions about what happened?"

She didn't look amenable to the request, but after Jude nodded she moved a couple of steps aside with Tyler. She'd have to tell them what happened eventually. Now was as good a time as any.

Jude shuddered at the thought of what might have happened if the team hadn't gotten there. If he hadn't woken up.

"Sorry," the EMT said as he dabbed the back of Jude's head with something.

Jude shrugged. It hurt, but it wasn't this man's fault and there was no use complaining. He saw Milsner, and waved the man over.

"Glad to see you're okay, Brauer." He glanced at the EMT. "He is okay, right?"

"I'm fine." Jude wouldn't accept anything less, not considering he was going to stay with Zoe. They still had to find Alan Reskin and everyone else who was involved before this was over.

The EMT said, "A doctor should probably be the one to draw that conclusion, my man. This is a nasty bump."

"Is it still bleeding?"

"No," the EMT said grudgingly. "But that doesn't mean you don't need checking out in a hospital. I'm not a doctor."

Jude stood up. He nearly swayed, but planted his feet. There was too much to do to sit there any longer.

"Hey."

He held up a hand to silence the EMT's protest, then said to the agent, "What's the latest?"

"We have Terrence in custody. Again." Milsner folded his arms. "And you can guarantee we aren't turning him over to PD after the colossal mess up last time."

Jude didn't think Terrence's escape was

entirely the fault of the detectives. But with the added security Terrence would no doubt have, this second time around there was no way he'd get away again. Everyone would be all the more aware of any threat of an ambush considering what had happened. The man was wily, and he wasn't working alone. Their only advantage was that Terrence didn't seem to be thinking rationally. He should have run, fled the city and gone into hiding. They might never have found him. Instead, Terrence had come back for Zoe again. He'd tried to kill all of them—himself included—and would have succeeded. So, was he just suicidal, or was there something else going on?

"Before the fire Zoe said she recognized the woman she saw killed," Jude said. "I confirmed with her what she was saying, and I think she was sure. She knows who it was, and you aren't going to believe it."

"Who'd she see killed?"

"Alan Reskin's wife." Jude let the words hang in the silence.

The agent's eyes widened.

"I know."

"But that's impossible," the agent said. "Reskin is missing, but I talked to Beatrice Reskin at her house a couple of hours ago. She's very much alive."

SIXTEEN

Even though she wasn't close enough to hear what was said, Zoe saw the look come over Jude's face, one of complete betrayal. And it was directed at *her.*

The police officer cleared his throat.

"I'm sorry." She glanced back at him, where he waited expectantly for her answer. "What was the question?"

"I asked if you're prepared to testify to everything you've told me. If we're going to bring Terrence Willis to justice, then we're going to need your help to do so."

Like she wanted the case to hinge on her. Surely they'd be able to gather evidence enough that her testimony wouldn't be so vital. Who knew where she would be, or what she'd be doing by the time the trial came around? She didn't want to have to put her entire life on hold until Terrence was sentenced.

"You don't look thrilled."

She granted him a smile, since he was being nice about it. "I'm not, but if it's important then I'll do it. I do want him brought to justice."

Tyler at least needed to see his mom doing what was right, not just what she wanted to do.

"Good." The officer nodded, as though he respected her answer. "It's your call, but it will certainly help. I could compel you to testify, though that isn't the preferred way to get a result in this."

She appreciated his candor, not wanting to be forced to cooperate. Just the memory of being marched into the living room with her son made her want to stand up and tell everyone what that killer had done. Terrence had terrorized her to the point where she didn't know if she'd sleep nightmare-free for the rest of her life. Jude had been knocked out, and she'd had to face the man alone. Forced to stand between Terrence and her son and play the role of protector that Jude was so good at.

It was amazing to know now that she could do it. Sure, she'd quaked in her seat. And walking had taken a conscious effort to lock her legs and keep standing, but she'd done it. From the panic room to the living room she'd held her head high and done what Jude would have—she'd protected her son under her own strength.

Or maybe it had been God giving her strength.

Agents walked Terrence out of the house then, his limp pronounced from where Jude had shot his leg, and the detective watched. Zoe didn't want to look, but it was part of facing down her fears. She held her head high—again—and watched them take Terrence to an SUV. He looked cowed, but she knew better. He'd shown no indication of remorse for anything he'd done, or any of the ways he'd harmed her and others. The man was her tormentor, and for weeks now he had made her life nothing better than a nightmare.

"It's over now." The realization hit her. Terrence had been brought in, and this time there was no way the team would let him get away. At least she hoped not.

Tyler hugged her side a little tighter.

"That it is," the officer said.

Jude was looking at the agents escorting Terrence as well, but he still had that scowl on his face. The one he'd directed at her.

The officer said, "It's over for him. The quicker he faces that fact, the better it will be for everyone." Was that pride in his department she could hear, or just wishful thinking? "The Secret Service will want to follow up, as well. I'm sure they'll be over to talk to you soon."

She nodded, though the thought of additional people wanting to talk to her made her feel even more exhausted as the adrenaline from the captive situation faded. Her head had begun to spin. Now she was jittery, and at the same time weirdly drained.

"I'll be sure to ask them how Terrence got the address to their supersecret safe house while we're talking." They had to have an explanation. Had Agent Steve Fronter somehow known before he tried to abduct her and gotten the word out?

With the exception of Jude, the Secret Service had been nothing to her but more problems she'd had to face. How could she trust them now, when they had put her in danger twice already?

"Now, ma'am—"

"Don't call me that." She wasn't old, and this wasn't the Victorian age. "My name is Zoe, and you know what? People keep telling me I'll be fine, that I'm 'safe now.' But I'm starting to think it's not true."

"You said yourself, it's over now."

"It isn't over."

Alan Reskin wanted her dead, and there was

nothing to stop him sending anyone else who would take the money to find her. To kill her, and probably Tyler, as well.

She squared her shoulders. "I want the police officers at the hospital to stay with my sister and Jude's father. You can't call them off now even though Terrence is in custody—it still isn't safe for them. They'll come after them."

"They aren't going to be—"

Jude cut off the police officer. "You need to take a breath, Zoe." His strides were long and purposeful as he closed the distance between them. He eyed Tyler pointedly and she realized she was freaking him out.

Her son was shaking in her arms.

"Ty…"

"Mom, what's wrong with you?"

She didn't even know.

"Your mom is having a panic attack."

One second she'd been fine, and now she could hardly breathe. Zoe pressed a hand to her chest, trying to draw in air. "What's…? I'm…"

He touched her shoulders, his face close. "Breathe. Concentrate on drawing air in. Push it out slowly between your lips."

She stared at his lips, full and red. She recalled the feel of them, pressed to hers.

Zoe realized the direction of her thoughts and coughed, then sucked in a breath.

"Good." He thought she was following his directions when instead she'd been staring at his lips. "When you're okay, we'll go. Get somewhere safe."

"Nowhere—" she breathed "—is safe." That sucking feeling came back, squeezing the air from her lungs. Her thoughts shut off and she couldn't even think through the sensation.

"You are safe. There's nothing to worry about." He hugged her and Tyler, his arms loose.

"The..." She couldn't even say it.

"Everything will be fine, Zoe. There's nothing for you to be so scared about."

She shook her head. Why did he think everything was fine?

"Mom?" Her son sounded panicked. She wanted to reach for him, to comfort him, but couldn't seem to move. Her legs folded and she dropped. Before she hit the ground, Jude swung her up into his arms and then she was moving. He felt good surrounding her, even with the twang of pain in her shoulder.

He was strong, and so much more capable than she was. One encounter with Terrence, one attempt at bravery, and now she was completely freaking out.

He set her on a stretcher in the ambulance. The EMT put a mask on her face, and cool air flooded her mouth and nose. Much better.

"Is she okay?" She felt her son's small hand clutch hers, warm but trembling.

"Yeah, Tyler." Jude's voice sounded far away. "She'll be okay." He also sounded sad when she wanted to see him smile. She wanted to fix what was awry for him, and force him to ditch that distance he'd placed between them in the kitchen. He'd been so closed off, and she wanted to know what real closeness between them would be like.

If it was even possible, Zoe wanted to know what forever would feel like.

Jude stared at her, lying on a stretcher in the ambulance. The juxtaposition of the scared gaze which had compelled him to protect her, and the fact that she hadn't seen a murder as she claimed, collided in his mind. Only the fact that while no one was dead the danger to Zoe's life had been very real stopped him from abandoning her completely. That, and the fact that Tyler was holding his hand, tethering him to this small family.

The EMT waved them in. "Let's go."

Tyler didn't move with him, so Jude leaned

in close. "Come on, buddy. Let's get your mom out of here."

The boy nodded, though he didn't look comforted. Even so, the idea of escaping this latest trauma must have overcome the fear keeping him static because he climbed into the ambulance and took a seat.

Jude sat beside him and rubbed the boy's back while they watched the EMT check Zoe's blood pressure and heart rate.

"Is she on any medication?"

Jude opened his mouth, then realized he didn't know the answer. "Pain meds for her shoulder, I have no idea about regular prescriptions. Tyler?"

"What?"

Did the boy even know what medication was? "Um…does your Mom go to the doctor?"

"No." He shook his head. "She's never sick."

"Maybe she had a cold one time, and never told you?"

"We have a chart because I got allergies. Now we count how many days with no sneezing, because that squirty stuff works."

Jude had no idea what that meant, but if they were counting healthy days it had to mean something. "And your mom? Does she sneeze?"

Tyler shook his head. "We went out for pizza to celebrate, because it's been fifteen months."

This was probably the weirdest conversation Jude had ever been a part of, but it was also cute. He figured parents cared about this stuff. If the worst Tyler was concerned about was allergies, and he and his mom were both clean, that was good.

He glanced at the EMT. "Does that help?"

"No, but it was pretty hilarious." The man was grinning, though it might've been more of a smirk. Jude couldn't tell. As far as he could see, nothing about this was even the slightest bit amusing. "I was going to tell you that you have a beautiful family, but I guess you're not related."

"We've only known each other for a couple of days."

The EMT gaped. "I thought you guys were together." He motioned between Jude and Zoe, who was watching the whole exchange with those wide green eyes but saying nothing. "And that he was your son."

Tyler looked at Jude, who said, "He isn't my son. But he is my friend."

The kid nodded, then said to the EMT, "Jude let me play in his tree house. He played in it when he was a kid, and it's *awesome*. There are eight steps up, and a balcony. The roof has a hole on one side where the squirrels get in, but Mr. Andrew is going to help me patch it."

Jude said, "He is?"

Tyler nodded at his question.

"I'll help, too. Maybe we can paint it, as well."

"Sweet. It's gonna be *epic*."

Jude grinned, and figured the kid got most of his vocabulary not from kids at school but from the internet. It was the favorite complaint of agents he worked with about their children. Using slang words they'd learned from YouTube so their parents had no idea what they were talking about. Since Tyler was only seven, this was likely the early stages of that very same problem.

Would Jude be around to see the next evolution of Tyler's development? He'd assumed he would be at one point. He'd certainly hoped for it. But if Milsner's suspicion was true and Zoe had been lying, how would Jude ever maintain his reputation? He would be the agent duped by the witness, who then let her stick around.

He figured she'd misunderstood what she saw that night. The woman could have been hurt, but not died. Or it might not have been Reskin's wife.

He'd thought Zoe would turn out to be the woman he wanted to spend the rest of his life with, but apparently that wasn't what God had for him. *What is it then, Lord? Because I'm confused. Why put her in my life if she's just going to turn out to be a fraud?* He'd tried to help her, because it was the right thing to do. But now he knew she hadn't seen what she'd claimed to, what was he supposed to think?

An unreliable witness was better than a lying one. Though not by much. Jude didn't want that for Zoe. She didn't need the stress of having her word—or her memory—questioned. She shouldn't have to doubt herself, and neither did he even want the slightest thought that he might not be able to trust her even entering his mind.

The one he felt really bad for was Tyler. The boy didn't deserve to be caught in the middle of this whole mess.

It would hurt them all when it was over; there was no denying that. And Jude didn't think he could do anything about it, either. He'd known he had to keep his distance, but he hadn't.

And now they were all going to suffer the consequences.

Jude would have to sever the ties. He was going to be ridiculed for a hunch that wound up with them catching a bad guy who had nothing to do with their case. Not a waste of time, but not part of their jobs, either.

Jude's phone rang. Zoe opened her eyes then, and glanced over at him. Jude looked away.

"Agent Brauer."

"Put her on the phone." The man's voice was gravelly, and one Jude didn't recognize.

"Who is this?" He wasn't just going to hand the phone over.

"I only talk to her."

Zoe sat up, tugging off the oxygen mask. "What is it?"

Jude mouthed, *He wants to talk to you.*

She reached for the phone. Jude didn't want to give it to her, but the man had made it clear he wouldn't answer Jude's questions.

He put the phone on speaker.

"Hello?" Her voice quaked.

"Guess I didn't work hard enough, since your sister is still alive."

Was that man's voice Alan Reskin? Jude didn't know.

"Though that just means I get to try again."

Her face paled. Zoe gasped. "No, I—"

"You meet with me. No cops, no feds. No funny business. Or that sister of yours? Your son or those church people? One of them will die."

SEVENTEEN

Zoe chewed on her lip as Jude drove out of the city on the freeway. It was just after two in the morning. She didn't even recognize the address the man on the phone had given her, or his voice. But Jude evidently knew where they were supposed to go.

After he issued that threat to Ember, to Tyler and to Jude's parents, she hadn't been able to focus on much else. Then it had taken time to get to the hospital, get checked out and leave Tyler with Leanne. Again. Zoe wanted her son to be with *her*, considering he was in danger wherever he was. But cops and Secret Service agents were at the hospital to make sure nothing happened to any of them.

The threat still scared her. Alan Reskin had proved his reach. Terrence had found her multiple times when it should have been impossible.

Zoe ran her hands down her face, then glanced over at Jude in the driver's seat.

He'd barely spoken to her since the call. Was he scared for his family? Did he wish he'd never met her? Zoe stared out the window trying to figure out how she was supposed to get through this without his support.

But she wanted to know what he expected from her in this meeting Reskin had demanded. "What do you—"

Jude held up a hand. "One second." Then he tapped the screen on the dash. The low murmur of the radio shut off and a phone began to ring.

He was making a call? Now? She'd only wanted to talk to him, but apparently that was too much to ask.

"Agent Daniels."

"It's Brauer, sir."

"Ah, good," the man replied. He sounded older and more refined, but there was a pleasant warmth to his voice. Like a wealthy uncle who disliked scuff marks on his wood floor and always kept a fully stocked candy dish in his office. "I followed up with the agents about their conversation with Beatrice Reskin. So I've been apprised as to the fact that Alan's wife is very much *alive* and wanting to know why there's a woman claiming she is dead."

Zoe gasped. "She's alive?" But...she'd seen her lying on the ground. Alan had hauled her up and into his car. There had been blood on her head.

The agent said, "Miss Marks." The man didn't sound the least bit pleased to hear from her. "Agents are accompanying you and Jude to the meeting place and will endeavor to keep the two of you safe. We aren't in the business of placing our agents in unnecessary danger. Nor will we put innocents at risk."

"She looked dead," Zoe choked out. "I saw her—"

"As soon as we locate Alan Reskin we'll be able to ask him ourselves why he sent his wife's cousin to terrorize you."

Zoe swallowed.

"Until then, she's claiming she has no idea what you're talking about, and he is missing."

She wanted to pray they caught him at this meeting. Hopefully before he killed her or harmed anyone else. Zoe didn't want Jude to get hurt—more—because of her.

She shook her head while her thoughts spiraled like a tornado. They thought she was lying. That had to be the reason why Jude had been so weird with her in the ambulance. That Secret Service agent at the scene must have told him Alan Reskin's wife was alive. He thought she had betrayed him, that she'd used him for protection.

Zoe was nearly sick at the idea he could think so low of her. He really thought she was so despicable?

And yet he was still here. He'd still promised her Tyler would be safe, which meant he was even more of a good man than she'd previously given him credit for. He was probably a better person than she was, since he had that Christian grace and love. How did she compete with a person so amazing? She could hardly live up to it.

The idea was depressing, but the rest of her life was a mess, so why not her love life, as well? Not that she loved Jude. It was just the idea of them being in a relationship was looking more and more impossible as she got to know him.

"Zoe?" The agent's voice boomed through the car's speakers and she realized she hadn't even been listening.

"I'm sorry, what did you say?"

"Terrence Willis has admitted his cousin's husband hired him to come after you. To scare you into leaving town."

"The last time I saw him…" She realized that wasn't accurate. "The time before, in the woods—" when Jude had saved her, and she'd been injured "—he said *she'd* changed *her* mind, and the order was to bring me in. But he was going to kill me. Save everyone the trouble, since he didn't believe I wasn't going to tell anyone what I saw. He said *she*."

"She, meaning his cousin—the woman you thought Alan killed? Think back to that night. What did you see, if the woman is alive?"

"I thought it was her murder," Zoe said. "I figured it was why they wanted me taken out of the equation. But if she isn't dead, then what *did* I see?" Maybe she'd witnessed something and made an assumption, not even realizing the truth—which was what they were trying to hide.

"I guess we'll find out when Alan Reskin is found."

She nodded, then realized he couldn't see her, and said, "Thank you." She knew they didn't necessarily want to help her, but what they did would mean she was free of this cat-and-mouse game her life had become.

Zoe said, "I know you aren't doing this for me, but I appreciate it. My son will be safe because of all of you." She glanced at Jude, just so he knew her gratitude was genuine.

Even if he hadn't believed her story—and she could see why he wouldn't, given the evidence—he had still done what he could to keep her and Tyler safe. How could she fault him for that, even if it meant they would part ways? She wanted a relationship with him, but could still keep things amicable if it didn't happen.

Later on, when she was alone, she would cry it out. She could never let Jude know how sad she'd be if nothing developed between them. But she would let him go. Jude was way too out of her league for it to work.

"Stay safe," the agent said. "We believe Alan might be desperate enough to do anything to cover up what he's hiding."

"Will do, sir," Jude said to him. "And tell the team I said thank you." He tapped the screen to end the call, and Zoe immediately jumped on the silence.

"That's why you were acting weird. Because she isn't dead, and you thought I was lying about having seen a murder."

He opened his mouth, and then closed it without saying anything.

Zoe folded her arms, which was actually quite painful to her injured shoulder, and huffed. "Don't bother to deny it."

"I didn't."

She huffed again. "Good." Maybe it was for the best they go their separate ways after this. If they tried for a relationship, they'd probably end up arguing like this for the rest of their lives. He'd never believe her, and she wouldn't want to stoop so low as to try to defend herself in order to change his mind.

Jude wanted to kiss that pouty set to her lips, but didn't think she'd be too amenable to it in her current mood. When they fought, how would he keep himself from laughing and then kissing her?

She would probably get even madder if he did that.

He was scared for his parents, for Tyler and Ember. But he was more worried about Zoe having to face Alan Reskin. Despite the backup, she would be in danger.

Jude took the turn for the meeting, and asked her, "What do you need to do with Alan?" He figured repeating it would get her mind off her frustration with him and back on what was about to happen if she went over it with him one more time.

Jude had some ideas of his own that he'd pitched to Daniels in an email. Right now Zoe and this meeting were his focus.

"Keep him on topic. Don't let him threaten me. Ask questions if I can." Her voice was quiet, and she stared out the window at the buildings on either side of the street instead of looking at him. "So we can figure this out."

She paused. "He might just plan to kill me and be done with it."

"He might." Jude hadn't wanted to mention the possibility to her, but it was one she needed to consider. He was glad she was doing so now.

She shifted then, straightening in her seat. "I could try to get him to say what happened, and what he's hiding. Though I can't believe Alan's wife is denying it when she was involved."

"Maybe it was someone who just looks a lot like her, or who was pretending to be her?" Jude thought more on it, then said, "Maybe she has a sister."

Zoe was quiet, so he glanced at her. "I already told Daniels. He's looking into it."

She looked mad again, not excited as she'd been at the prospect of getting Alan to talk.

"Zoe—"

She looked away from him. "Now I don't even know what I thought. But I'm mixed up in something, and it's got Tyler, Ember and your parents' lives on the line. Even if they're safe the Secret Service will probably just arrest me for being part of it even when I have no idea what *it* even is."

"That isn't—"

"Thanks, but no thanks," she said, derision

in her voice. "I don't think I need any help. Not if you're just determined to think badly of me no matter what."

Jude pulled up short of the building they were supposed to be at in fifteen minutes for the meeting that would hopefully end all this back-and-forth. He shoved the gear shift to Park and turned in his seat to face her.

"Enough." He scratched his head, wanting instead to tear out his hair. "We need to focus. This is about Alan Reskin, not about you and me and whatever you *think* is going on right now. You saw what you saw—you didn't have all the information. We still don't know exactly what happened."

He took a breath. She didn't meet his gaze, just stared out the windshield. He said, "In the meantime, this man has sent his wife's cousin after you, and is threatening our families. I'm guessing he was the one who found Tyler in the tree house and sent you that message. Unless we do this right, these people are going to keep coming after you. So for everyone's sake maybe you could push aside your worries about the Secret Service and do this with me."

Her mouth moved, like she was torn between a full-on pout and biting her lip. Before she could argue some more with him, Jude said, "Now let's get set up."

She opened her door, so he did the same and jogged to meet her on her side. "Stop." He held up one hand. "You shouldn't have gotten out without waiting for me." He held out one hand, the other on the small of her back, leading her to the rear of the SUV.

"I wasn't really in the mood to wait for you."

"You need to get in the mood, Zoe. Because the alternative is Tyler loses his mom." It was the reality of the threat against her. "This could be a trap. Which means you need to put aside your feelings and *listen to what I say.* I know what I'm doing."

"Fine." She lifted her chin.

Jude didn't figure that meant she'd give him more than the tiniest bit of leeway. She wasn't about to relinquish her anger. But she would have to figure out how to either ignore him, or put it aside until later. The woman needed to focus, despite the stress and the pain, or they wouldn't get safely through this.

He lifted the rear door and had her sit for a minute while he slid a protective vest over to her. She should probably wear a helmet as well, but there hadn't been time to get one. They'd barely made it here—and only had minutes to spare now—before they had to be inside the building.

Jude checked his weapon and then holstered it.

"Do I get one of those?"

"No."

That so-cute lip curled up. "Too bad. It looks good on you, so I figure it will make me look less like a bedraggled mess."

She thought that? "What does Alan care how you look? Trying to impress him?"

She shot him a look, like he was the dumbest man she'd ever met.

"Or not." He didn't understand her at all. "We're supposed to be focusing." He secured his radio and stuck the earpiece in. "Lone Star, this is Choirboy. Do you copy?"

The voice returned, "We copy you loud and clear, Choirboy."

Zoe laughed. "Choirboy?"

Jude shrugged. "Pastor's kid."

The smile on her face was cute—and completely distracted his focus from what was ahead.

"Come on." He waved her off the rear of the SUV so he could shut the door. When he did so, he said, "We don't have much time."

She walked with him, but didn't let it go. "We aren't going to talk about what that was? For a second it looked like you were going to kiss me."

Could he even define what had birthed that desire in him? Jude couldn't resist saying, "Would you have let me?"

Zoe shook her head. "You should know the answer to that by now. Even if everything else is messed up."

He went first, holding his shotgun—because why carry one gun when he could carry two—and led the way into the building, a metal walkway cutting the room in half horizontally. Some kind of manufacturing warehouse.

It was quiet inside, maybe even deserted. Jude moved slowly, scanning the area. He didn't see anyone.

A tiny movement up above them, at the far end of the room, drew his attention.

Before he could react, shots rang out.

Jude dived, taking Zoe down with him. At the last second before they hit the concrete floor he heard, "Shots fired!"

EIGHTEEN

Before Zoe even knew what happened Jude's body slammed into hers and they were flying through the air. Gunshots cracked across the room and pinged into the concrete wall behind where they'd been standing only a second ago.

She hugged Jude's body as they hit the ground and rolled, her on top for a second and then him. His big frame shielded her, but that only meant he was the one who was left exposed. She knew how that felt, and she didn't want it to happen to him. She held him tight in her arms, her grip secure as she prayed, "Jesus, please!"

Not that she even knew what words to say, but wouldn't He know even if she couldn't form more words? He was powerful, and He had saved her—she could admit as much now; otherwise she'd have been dead long before this. She had no doubt in her mind He could do it again now. And in return, Zoe would give serious consideration to this whole "church" thing. It couldn't be denied that God just kept saving her—using Jude to do it.

Secret Service agents poured in the door. One even came through a window. The yells were blurred words, and she realized her ears were ringing, but there were no more gunshots. Zoe let go of Jude long enough to stick her fingers in her ears and wiggle to try to get some hearing back. Like she could jog the ability loose.

Jude grasped her hands and mouthed something.

Zoe said, "What?"

He said it again, but she couldn't understand more other than it looked like he said *Eyebrower Rifle*. He drew her hands down, though, so she left her ears alone. The ringing was still there.

He got off her and rolled to the side. Zoe sat up and saw agents pin a man to the floor, his face mushed against the dusty concrete. They got him secured and up on his feet fast, like complete professionals. They hadn't wasted any time taking care of the threat.

One picked up the huge gun the man had been firing. *High-powered rifle*. As they walked him across the building, right past her, she realized that's what Jude had mouthed.

The man looked familiar, though he wasn't her former boss. Who was trying to kill her now? She certainly didn't want to add another man to the list, but since Terrence had been captured by the Secret Service, Alan Reskin— or his wife—could have sent this man. The whole meeting had been a ruse. He hadn't wanted to talk to her, and now they had lost their shot to capture him.

Alan was still at large.

Zoe slumped against the wall.

Jude leaned over to her. "Are you okay?"

She made out his voice over the ringing, and nodded. She was exhausted and in pain from the jar to her shoulder wound. Would she ever just be able to rest and let the thing heal? It felt like this would be her life now. Minutes stretched into days, terror lacing every second of it as she fought for some semblance of normality in this craziness.

Can You help with that as well, Lord? Wasn't peace His thing? She could certainly use some of that right now, and it would likely start with speaking to her son and assuring herself he was okay. When she could actually hear well enough to make a call, she was going to ask Jude if she could borrow his phone.

A Secret Service agent, the one Jude had been speaking to outside the safe house, strode over. Jude helped Zoe stand, and she leaned on him. More for comfort than because she needed the support. He had saved her life, and whatever weirdness was between them, he was a good man. One who was too good for her.

Could they still be friends? She didn't want to live with a broken heart, wondering what could have been while he found someone better than her. But she did want him in her life.

He wrapped his arm across her lower back, and she put her head on his shoulder.

The agent said, "Are you both okay?"

Her hearing was getting better. "I'm okay."

She felt Jude's nod brush against the top of her head. "Me, too. And for the record, the shooter is Alan Reskin's head of security."

Zoe gasped, then spun to look at the man. Jude was right. She'd seen that man at work.

"This guy is just digging his grave deeper by trying to kill both of us." His arm around her waist tightened. "Reskin should've been here. We should have gotten him. Instead he's just making things worse for when we do catch up to him."

"He is." The agent nodded. "And it looks like he was never here." He glanced at Zoe. "You were lured here with the threat to your families, probably so his man could kill you."

She'd figured she was the one they wanted to silence.

"He's ex-military," Jude said.

The other agent didn't like that much. "I'll pull his record."

Federal agents all seemed to be a breed of man the likes of which she'd never met. Zoe couldn't imagine being as noble as Jude, as self-assured. It was probably part of Secret Service training, but she didn't think it would lessen the longer she knew any of them. It was likely they would just keep impressing her even more.

The agent studied her, then smiled. "What is it?"

Zoe shook her head. Jude shifted her so he could see her face, then said, "You okay?"

"Can I borrow your phone? I want to check on Tyler."

He pulled it out. "I can't believe it's not even cracked or anything." He swiped at the screen, and when he handed it to her said, "It's already dialing my mom."

"Thanks." Zoe put the phone to her ear and stepped away so they could talk and she'd still be able to hear Leanne.

"Jude? Is that you?"

"It's Zoe, actually. Did you want to speak to him? I was just wondering how Tyler is doing." More words wanted to come out, but she halted them to give Leanne a second to speak. What was it with adrenaline making her want to talk a mile a minute?

"Tyler..." Her voice was shaky.

Dread filled Zoe as she said, "Leanne. What happened to Tyler?" Hearing the shift in her tone, Jude and the agent moved toward her, and she felt Jude's comforting touch on her shoulder. But she couldn't relax into it. "Leanne?"

Jude took the phone. "What happened?" His face paled as he listened. Then he said, "Do that." He hung up. "Tyler was taken. The cops showed her a few photos and Mom identified the man as Alan Reskin. He hit her over the head, but she saw him for a second. He took Tyler from the hospital."

She couldn't even think. "He took Tyler?"

Jude glanced at the agent. "This was a distraction."

Zoe's mouth gaped. "What?"

"He lured us here so he could take Tyler while we were busy fending off the shooter."

"I'll make some calls and find out who is running point." Agent Milsner took a step back, then glanced at Zoe. "I will keep you informed, okay?"

She nodded, though Jude was unsure she'd actually understood what the man said to her. When he'd left them alone, Jude said, "What do you need?"

She shook her head, glanced at the ceiling and bit her lip.

He wanted to gather her into his arms, but was that going to help? She seemed restless, like she needed to move. "Let's go outside."

He led her to the night air, his arm around her shoulders. She was tense, like she was ready to bolt at any second. He wanted her to stay with him, to lean on him as she had done so many times already. Instead, he found himself caught up in her tension.

Jude pictured the boy in his mind, and fear moved through him like the first tremors of an earthquake even as he tried to be reassuring. "They'll get him back."

She didn't say anything.

When he stopped on the sidewalk, Zoe looked at him. "What are we doing?"

"What do you mean?"

"We need to *go*. Like to the hospital."

He shook his head. "Tyler isn't there anymore, and we would just be in the way."

"Then what are we waiting for? Shouldn't we be doing something?"

"I know it feels like that, but we have to wait

for Agent Milsner to find us with the information. Or Alan will call us. He's contacted you before."

She nodded. "On your phone. To schedule this *fake* meeting." Her hands balled into fists, and her jaw clenched. "Now we have to just wait? I don't know if I can even do that."

"It might not be long before he calls—" Jude didn't know for sure, but what else could he say? "—to ask for a ransom."

"And the longer the wait is, the greater the chance that he just kills Tyler." Tears rolled down her face.

Jude gathered her into his arms. "He needs Tyler alive in order to use him against you. It serves nothing to hurt him." Unless he was deranged, which was always a chance. But Jude was going to pray—and keep praying—that Tyler would be found, alive and well. *I'm asking, Lord. Seeking and knocking. And I'm not going to stop until he's here with us.*

He rubbed up and down her back, even while fear drove his actions. The movement was nervous, he knew. Maybe she wouldn't notice, though. "The Secret Service can track my phone. They can find him."

The last time Alan had called, to set the meeting, the techs had tried to trace it, but Alan had turned off his phone before they could locate it. If they kept him on the phone long enough, and the Secret Service was ready, hopefully this time they'd be able to track him down.

And get Tyler back.

Zoe cried, and he switched to praying aloud. It seemed to help her.

"Brauer."

He glanced up, but didn't let go of Zoe.

Milsner strode over. "Let's go back to the office. We have the setup there, and you guys can get cleaned up."

Jude nodded. They were covered in dust from the floor. As they walked to the car he said to Zoe, "Do you need more meds?"

She winced. "My shoulder is killing me, but I don't think I even care right now."

He still planned to have a doctor called in to check her out. His head was seriously pounding as it was.

Jude was going to personally make sure Tyler was found safe and returned to his mom. He just wasn't going to promise Zoe. Not if there was a chance he might not succeed. *God, I'm trusting You in this. Help me know what to do.* He prayed the emotional turmoil on her and her son wasn't so bad they couldn't have normal lives after it was over.

And it would be over. Soon.

He helped her into her seat in the car, and since he figured it would hurt her shoulder to buckle up he did that for her, as well. When he leaned back, he studied her face. Everything he saw was precisely what he expected. It just didn't make him feel better. She was scared for her son's life, and he admitted it to himself then that he was, as well. He just wasn't about to let her know that. She thought of him as the hero who was never afraid or unsure—he wouldn't ruin that image for her.

"Thank you."

He touched her cheek as softly as her tone had been when she'd said those two simple words. "You're very welcome, Zoe." He stood quietly for a second, tracing his thumb over her cheekbone. She was a beautiful woman, one he was proud to know. Her strength and vulnerability had both seen her through this.

Jude couldn't believe he'd ever doubted her for a second, but figured it was his insecurities talking and not logic. He wanted to trust her. Just as he wanted her to trust him.

"This will be over soon. And years from now, when Tyler is the star of his football team and you're fielding phone calls from girls every night of the week because they all want him to be their boyfriend—" She started to smile, and he knew he was on the right track. "You're barely going to remember this time in your life except as a blip. A brief period where things weren't about whether he's going to be safe driving his own car, or if he should be allowed to stay out past midnight on the weekend."

"The answer to that one is *no*." Her smile was small, but it was there. "I don't care how old he is, or whose house the party is at."

"That's my girl." Jude touched his lips to hers.

She blinked. Surprised at his words, or his kiss? He closed the door and rounded the car, not even sure himself which one it was.

His phone rang as he climbed in. He looked at his phone and then glanced back, out the door to the vehicle behind, where Milsner was in his car. Jude lifted his hand, thumb and pinky out, to indicate his phone. Milsner nodded. Jude started the engine and connected it through the Bluetooth.

"I think this is him." He turned to Zoe. "Ready?"

"No, but do I have a choice?"

He squeezed the back of her neck and then touched the screen to answer the call, not wanting to wait much longer or it would go to voice mail. Zoe said, "Yes?" Her voice shaky.

"So you finally pick up. I don't like waiting." Jude didn't recognize the man's voice, but this for sure wasn't some friendly wrong number. "You want the kid, you meet me at Liberty Park."

Jude pulled an old receipt from the center console along with a pen he prayed worked and quickly scrawled a note.

The man continued, "The corner of 1300 S and S 700 E at six in the morning. You come alone, no cops. No feds. And no tricks, or your little boy is dead."

Jude held up the note. Zoe's brow furrowed as she read, and then said, "I want proof of life, or I tell the world what I know."

"*What you know.* That's rich. You don't even know what you know, that's your problem." He laughed. "But I'll give you what you want. As a show of good faith that you will reciprocate by following my instructions. To. The. Letter."

There was a shuffle on the other end of the phone, and the Tyler's voice came on. "Mom?"

"Tyler, I'm here!"

"Mom!"

"I'm coming to get you, honey. I love you so much."

"I love you, too, M—" The rustle returned.

"How sweet," the man said in a dark tone. "Liberty Park. One hour."

He hung up.

NINETEEN

Zoe walked faster than normal even though they were back at the office. There wasn't time to be slow. The clock was ticking to the meeting. Jude opened the door, and she followed him inside. There was one window, and it filled that whole wall. On the other side two agents were questioning Terrence Willis.

"Normally you wouldn't be allowed in here," Jude explained, "but in this case I'm not going to let you out of my sight."

That should have comforted her, but Zoe couldn't let any warmth in. Not right now, when her son was who knew where with a madman. Scared. Upset. Wondering if he was going to die, or whether Zoe and Jude would come and get him.

Even thinking about Jude's sweetness—his kiss—didn't help. She couldn't let those memories distract her.

Terrence's voice came through a speaker. "Told you already. I don't know."

"We think you do."

Terrence huffed.

Zoe glanced at Jude, whose frown was firmly directed at Terrence. "How long do we have?"

She had no watch and no phone, but there was a clock on the wall. Still, she needed to ask the question. She needed Jude to know the answer, as well.

He pulled out his phone and looked at the time. "One hour, forty-two minutes." He'd driven probably faster than he should have back to the office.

"And what are we waiting here for?" She motioned toward Terrence with a wave of her hand.

"We need to know if he admits or reveals anything." He balled his hands into fists. "The team is tearing apart Reskin's life."

"Thank you." At his look of surprise, she continued., "It's nice to know I'm not the only one going crazy. You can go to work if you want. You don't have to—"

"I want to be with you."

"But they're investigating, and I know I can't be part of it…"

He hugged her. She'd have preferred he kiss

her the way he had a couple of times already. Now wasn't the time, though. "You really aren't alone, Zoe. I want to be here with you." His squeeze was quick before he released her and concentrated again on what Terrence was saying.

Zoe understood the fact that it was time to be quiet, though doubts still rolled through her mind. The task force were all preparing for the "operation," as they were calling it. She was supposed to face down Alan Reskin and get back her son, and they were going with her.

When she'd helpfully pointed out the fact that Alan had said no cops and no feds, Jude had shaken his head. None of them were willing to even concede their presence could put her son in harm's way. They simply believed with everything they were that her son would be safer if they went against Alan's instructions and came anyway.

Zoe was seriously grateful for the grade-A backup she was going to have, but couldn't help wondering what Alan would do when he realized she'd defied his orders.

Jude had simply said, "You didn't agree to do what he said. He stated his demands, assuming you would comply, but he isn't counting on the task force showing up. And if he is, then we can watch for that as well because he'll have a contingency plan in place."

Zoe didn't want to think what Alan's plan was. Especially considering the plan likely involved killing her, and then her son.

One of the agents interviewing Terrence said, "Alan Reskin stated that Zoe didn't know *what* she knew." He paused. "Now, what do you think that means?"

Terrence shrugged. "How would I know?"

The agent studied him without saying anything.

"Fine. He's into what he's into. Doesn't mean it has anything to do with me."

"So you'll cut and run now to save yourself?"

Terrence sneered. "Better than being a rat. Isn't that what you people do? Flip the low man and get him to spill all the higher-ups."

"Then we should be especially amenable in this case. What with you being the *low man* and all."

That gave Terrence pause. Zoe watched him assess the agent, probably trying to figure out why he'd said that. He hadn't exactly been berating Terrence, but he certainly hadn't said good things, either.

Terrence said, "You wouldn't be able to unravel the whole thing even if I told you what I know."

"So this is a waste of time, then." The agent got up, and his partner who'd been sitting beside him did the same.

Jude leaned over. "They're impatient."

"They are?"

He nodded. "They don't like it that Reskin has Tyler any more than we do."

Zoe studied the agents. They looked cool and calm enough, but it made her feel better to know they cared.

The agents got to the door before Terrence said, "You don't want to hear what I know?"

"You just said it isn't the whole picture."

"But I can give you intel." His voice and demeanor all now screamed *desperate*.

"The woman Alan Reskin wants. What does she know that she shouldn't have found out about?"

Terrence gritted his teeth.

This man had been prepared to kill her and Tyler—and himself—so she didn't think he was going to be helpful. Still, she prayed they got a result. And fast.

It was almost time to leave.

"Not what. *Who* she shouldn't have found out about."

"Reskin's wife, your cousin?" The agent's words mirrored her thought.

Was all this because of the woman's identity, and not because Zoe thought she had witnessed a murder? Her brain spun with the possibilities. She'd been mistaken all along because the woman hadn't been dead, the way she thought. But now all this was because Reskin wanted to keep her identity a secret? That didn't make any sense. They knew Beatrice was his wife, so what was the big secret?

"It has to be more than that," Jude whispered.

The agents left Terrence alone in the interview room and trailed into the viewing room where they were. "Not a colossal waste of time, but not much better than that, either."

Zoe said nothing.

"I'm going to inform Agent Daniels what we know. If the operation goes as planned then Alan will be ours to question soon." The agent glanced at Zoe. "And your son will be safe."

She nodded, grateful for their concern. Any certainty she had right now was more of a prayerful hope than anything else. She was going to keep praying until Tyler was in her arms and they were both safe.

Jude took her hand. "Time to go."

The agent nodded, and she and Jude left the

room. He didn't waste time getting her outfitted with what she would need, and then drove her over to Liberty Park. She'd liked walking through it before, but after today she wondered if she would ever want to set foot here again. Even if they all came out unscathed—the best-case scenario—it didn't mean the memories of fear and danger wouldn't be strong forever.

Zoe bit her lip and kept praying. When Jude parked the car, he took her hand again and said a prayer of his own out loud asking for safety and protection. And justice.

He had her sit on the edge of the trunk and wired her up so they could hear her. "You don't have to raise your voice. Just talk normally like I'm doing now and we'll be able to hear you."

She nodded.

"I know this is going to be difficult, but you need to act as naturally as possible. The longer it is before he realizes the entire task force is here, the better."

She nodded again, and he leaned down to kiss her forehead.

"Okay?"

Zoe said, "Okay."

"I'm proud of you, Zoe."

She lifted her gaze to his.

"I'm *so* proud of everything you've done.

You're a strong woman who loves her son, and I get the feeling you'd do anything to protect the people you love."

She didn't let go of his gaze. "I would." Hopefully he would see the truth behind her words. That she would do anything to protect him, just as he would for her. Because she loved Jude. Whether he felt the same, or not.

Whatever he saw, it caused him to say, "Zoe—"

His words were interrupted by the radio. Agent Milsner said, "The task force is in place."

He'd been about to say it. He loved her, and Jude was pretty sure she loved him. But now wasn't the time to exchange those words. Not until he got her son back. He mentally thanked Milsner for his timing, and held Zoe's hand as they made their way through Liberty Park to the meeting point.

He would only walk part of the way with her, and then he would have to watch her put herself in danger while Jude figured out how to get her son. Alan Reskin would be distracted, and Jude was going to use it to his advantage.

He kissed her before they parted, putting into it everything he felt but hadn't been able to say. When he pulled back, pink flushed her cheeks.

Jude said, "I'll see you soon, okay?"

She gripped his elbows, leaned up on her tiptoes and pressed her lips to his. But she didn't kiss him. Zoe whispered, "I love you," against his lips. The movement was a tickle of feeling as gentle as butterfly wings.

Then she was gone.

Jude's stomach clenched as she walked away. He wanted to go with her, but knew there was nothing he could do. Alan had to believe there was no one there with Zoe or Tyler would be in even more danger than he already was.

Jude crept to his designated spot and watched, praying this was the correct end of the street where Alan would arrive, bringing Tyler with him. He couldn't help wondering what exactly Alan was into—or perhaps there were so many things it would be easier to list what he *wasn't* involved in. Was he the head of a criminal empire? It was possible.

What that had to do with his wife not being dead was also a mystery. What had happened that night in the parking lot? Zoe had seen the woman get hit. She'd fallen.

Little of this made sense, but so long as Tyler and Zoe were safe, then he could go back to work and run down the investigation. Eventually they would get to the bottom of what it was; it was just a matter of time.

Minutes later a Town Car pulled up at the curb. In the driver's seat was a blonde woman in pink. Alan climbed out of the front passenger side. Was the extra person his wife? He couldn't see well enough. If it was, and she was involved, then she was squarely implicating herself in what was happening by being here now.

In the back sat a smaller person, probably Tyler, though Jude couldn't see well enough from this position. All he could see was a head of red-blond hair, mussed like the boy's usually was. The two adults exchanged words through the open passenger door, and then Alan nodded. Taking orders from her?

He strode away, leaving Tyler with the woman.

Jude radioed in his position and the fact that he had eyes on Tyler.

Zoe had never been so scared in her life. She stood so still it probably looked like she had a bomb attached to her vest and she was frightened to move even a muscle. But he would see her, out in the open like this, even though the sun hadn't risen yet. The tree cover was set back, and there was nothing but open air and a path through the grass between her and the corner where 1300 S met S 700 E.

He scanned the area as he walked toward her, holding a gun. She tried to muster up courage, but the reality was that terror for her son—and the idea Alan might kill her and Tyler would end up an orphan—was the only thing she could think about.

The recognition was clear. He knew exactly who she was, despite the fact that he had only seen her either in passing or from a distance. He held the gun pointed at her.

"Where is my son?" The shake in her voice betrayed her nervousness, but she held her head high and faced him down.

"He is close by."

"What do you want?"

His gaze narrowed. He wasn't a particularly imposing man, but he wore his power like another one of his pricey suits. His hands looked manicured, and his haircut was likely expensive, but he'd run his hands through it at some point and so now it was in disarray. He was stressed? That was rich, considering he'd threatened to kill *her* son.

Alan said, "You will accompany me to the car. When you are inside, I will release your son. He can run off, but you will remain."

260 Witness in Hiding

"Bring him out here."

"No. He stays in the car. No interference from the Secret Service agents I know you have all around us." He looked both ways, like he knew there were task force agents stationed all over the park and neighboring streets. Which there were.

In fact, the van where they were running surveillance was parked across the street on the side Alan had walked over from. Had he noticed them there? Would they intercept her when she went that way with this man? She would go. Despite her argument, Zoe was going to do what she needed to in order to save her son.

Even if that meant making the ultimate sacrifice.

"Walk toward me, slowly. *Now.*"

She nearly jumped at his tone, but started toward him as instructed. When she was close enough, his arm snaked out and wrapped around her waist. He held the gun to her side, just above where the vest ended under her arm. Right against her skin. She choked out a breath and tried to think.

Where was Jude? Did he have Tyler; was her son safe? She could pray this would all be over before it even started, but was it too late for that? Alan would kill her if anyone came near them.

Zoe watched the bushes for agents, hiding and watching. Where were they? Maybe they were so good she couldn't see them, but how was that supposed to be reassuring?

Alan walked her to the sidewalk that ran down the length of the street and he twisted her body. Passersby had been cleared, but cars still drove down the street even this early. None could see the gun, though. Not from this angle.

One of the cars parked on the street had its driver's door open. Was that where they were headed? And where was Tyler?

Jude said, "Give him to me."

"Back up!" Beatrice Reskin—he'd been right about her identity when the car pulled up—waved the gun around like she had no idea how to use it, which was more dangerous than someone who'd taken a class in weapons.

"No way." She pulled Tyler in front of her, motioning to Jude. "Back away from the car."

Agents emerged from the shadows and out from behind trees. At least four men, though there were likely more she could see behind him.

Beatrice didn't even seem to notice.

"Don't hurt him." He had to say it. That was a very real possibility right now. As soon as he'd announced himself, stood right beside her open window, she'd turned almost feral and screamed at him to get back. The woman was prepared to fight to defend herself from whatever it was she'd gotten into, and Jude wasn't prepared to risk Tyler. He'd backed off, but she'd seen the approaching agents and was now using Tyler as a shield.

"Just let him go—he's innocent." As he said it, his eyes locked on Tyler's. The spitting image of his mom's, the same wide gaze that made Jude want to hang up everything and swoop the kid away to safety. He would give up the career he'd built all these years. His parents. His ministry. All of it meant nothing if Tyler and Zoe weren't in his life.

Beatrice turned back to the car and saw armed agents between her and the vehicle.

The boy whimpered, but Beatrice simply dragged him closer to where Jude had been hiding instead. Into the park. Was she waiting for Alan to return? No one had even announced the fact that Alan had shown up to meet Zoe.

Jude squared his aim. "Unless you let that boy go and put the gun down, you will die here."

"You can't kill me!" She screamed. "I'm Beatrice Reskin!"

What did her identity have to do with it? "Let the boy go, and I'll see about not adding attempted murder to the charges. Just kidnapping, along with the rest of it."

"I only did what was *necessary*. And it's over now. I've taken care of everything." Her determination, her certainty, caused more fear to spring to life inside him. She was holding a gun on a child, and still seemed convinced she hadn't done anything wrong. There was no reasoning with someone like that. And it would be no easy task to talk her down.

She waved the gun around some more. "The mayor *and* the district attorney will be hearing about this injustice!"

Her eyes widened, and he figured she'd noticed the arrival of yet more backup.

Jude said, "You thought we'd send Zoe alone?"

She opened her mouth, but a man yelled, "Beatrice!" Alan strode into view on the sidewalk where their car was parked, Zoe pressed against his side. From where he was positioned, Jude could see the gun pointed at Zoe's side. But Alan was paying no attention to her. He stared at Beatrice like the woman was crazy and he had no idea what she was doing. "Shouldn't we go?"

"I make the calls. Not you."

"It's time to leave!" Alan yelled.

Beatrice moved with Tyler back to where Alan held on to Zoe. They were going to take both of them? He needed to stop them—but he couldn't get a shot.

"Does anyone have an angle?" Pretense was out the window now. He wanted this done.

"No shot."

"No shot."

Beatrice was using Tyler's body as cover, and no one had a good angle that wouldn't risk the boy's life.

Beatrice fired toward Jude. It was so erratic, it missed anything vital. The second shot didn't, though, and he heard a scream. Pain sliced across the right side of Jude's neck and he fell back with the force of it. He brought his gun up, uncaring about the sting or the fact that he was likely bleeding a scary amount. Tyler was in the way still. He couldn't get a shot off without Zoe or her son getting hit in the process.

Tyler yelled. Zoe screamed, and the boy ran toward Jude.

"Leave him!" Alan shoved Zoe into the car and Beatrice flung her door open.

A shot rang out.

Tyler collided with him, his knees slamming into Jude's chest as the boy reached where he lay.

"I winged her." That was Milsner.

Jude was just glad no one had shot Zoe by accident. He grasped Tyler's hand, but could do nothing except watch as Zoe was driven away by the two criminals. Half the task force raced to get their cars and follow Alan and Beatrice.

The rest of the task force were headed his way, judging by the noise of boots racing toward Jude and Tyler. But he didn't care about who or why. Zoe was gone, and Jude was mad. He hadn't been able to protect her, and neither had any of his colleagues. Jude turned the full force of his ire on the men who should have protected him and his family.

Yes, they were his family.

"We're—"

It didn't matter what Milsner was about to say. Jude didn't need reassurance; he needed Zoe.

"Go get her back."

TWENTY

Zoe sat up from where they'd tossed her onto the backseat and hugged her middle. Alan Reskin had thrown her back here just like he'd done to that body—the not-actually-dead body of the woman who now sat beside him in the front seat. She could hardly believe it. Jude had said Beatrice was alive, but seeing it for herself was an entirely different thing. She was here. Injured. Mad.

But it was Alan who said, "No one will find out." He spewed the words out in a higher-pitched voice than he'd used before. "Once we get rid of *her* no one will ever know." His voice switched to what was his normal tone. "That's what you said, and now the entire Secret Service is going to be after us. They got involved. Like I *told you* they were going—"

Beatrice slapped him across the face with a bloody hand. "Shut up."

Zoe gasped.

Beatrice said, "I'm trying to think past this *stupid* gunshot wound and all your yammering isn't helping. Just give me some peace. The gall of them. Shooting me. Me!"

Zoe pulled at the door handle, her other hand ready to unclip her seat belt. She didn't care if they were going forty-five, winding between cars through downtown. Road rash was preferable to whatever Beatrice and Alan planned to do with her once they got wherever it was they were going.

"This whole thing is *your* fault."

Alan sneered. "Your plan. *Your* fault."

"If you hadn't been so stupid—" Her words were like venom, stealing whatever gave Alan the strength to face her down when he was obviously otherwise a kowtowed husband to this alpha female.

Beatrice threw her weight around as though she was born entitled to everyone's respect, but that wasn't how it was earned. Jude wasn't the kind of man who demanded respect or assumed it was his just because of his job. He simply acted like the good man he was, and it made her love him for it. No pretense. No manipulation. Everything in her yearned for Jude. His strength. The simple peace he carried with him. Was that because of his faith?

God, I would like some of that, as well. It

had been so long, it felt like starting over. *I'd like to know how to be like that, because he is everything so naturally. He just possesses it somehow and I want it, too.*

There was no audible voice in reply, but Zoe felt better all the same. She had to believe God was on her side because that was what faith was. She knew as much, despite what had happened these past few weeks. Sometimes seeing was believing, but it was far more powerful knowing the hope driving her was born of what she couldn't see. Couldn't touch or feel. She just had to *trust*. And she would.

Alan shrank in his seat, even as he drove them through the city. Beatrice yammered on and on about how everything was his fault, even though she'd told him to be quiet so she could think. In the end she let out a cry of frustration and slumped back into her seat.

"The virus took care of the files. Now all we have to do is get rid of her." Beatrice jabbed between the seats with her thumb extended.

Great. They were going to kill Zoe? Surely Jude was right behind them, following. Ready to rescue her.

Zoe turned in the seat, ignoring the pull of the stitches in her shoulder. There were cars behind, but no SUVs she recognized. Wasn't he coming? Despair threatened her faith that

God would send Jude to rescue her. What if he was too badly hurt and couldn't come? Tyler could be hurt, though she hadn't seen it happen. Zoe didn't want to think about either of them being injured, but there had to be a reason he wasn't behind her.

There had to be.

"What about the Secret Service?" Alan asked. "They have to know about the money."

"Eventually maybe, but before then you'll already be on your way to the White House. There will be nothing to stop our rise to the top." Beatrice fisted her hand and lifted it to shoulder height, punching the air. "We will be the most powerful couple in the world and no one will be able to do anything."

The woman was certifiable. Zoe couldn't believe what she'd just heard. "You're going to run for president?"

Beatrice shifted. "Not me." She motioned to her husband with a dismissive wave. "Him."

Alan didn't react. Zoe figured he was used to being dismissed. She almost felt sorry for him, living with a woman who was not only nuts but dragged everyone with her in it. He'd told Tyler in the tree house that he wanted out. The Secret Service would have probably helped him if he'd turned himself in, right? Yet he hadn't; he'd kidnapped Tyler and now Reskin was going along with the plan to kill Zoe just to pacify his insane and overbearing wife.

The brief surge of sympathy she had for him was short-lived. He was in charge of his own life, and yet he'd given his power to a wife who bullied him at every turn.

"I'll take care of the Secret Service," Beatrice said. "Don't worry about that." She patted her husband's arm, and Zoe saw the muscle twitch in his jaw that said Alan didn't welcome the contact. "I have everything in hand. You were wearing a mask. No one saw me hit that old man, or set that house on fire. The DA will believe anything I say."

"Except for the part where I have no intention of being the president." Alan's words were hard, but had no strength.

"So you said. As well as hitting me so I fell onto that dirty parking lot ground." Beatrice shook her head. "Disgusting."

"I told you I'm sorry about that," he said. "I was just so mad."

Zoe gaped. This man deferred to her without even thinking. He was apologizing for getting mad and punching her when she felt she could freely strike him with no recourse. Both of them needed counseling.

Beatrice huffed. "You're the biggest imbecile I've ever seen. Putting me in the back of the car. She thought I was dead! No wonder I had to send my cousin to find out what she was going to do."

"You could have gone yourself," Alan muttered. "But that would have involved lifting a finger."

She continued like he hadn't even spoken. "That idiot drew way too much attention to himself. Then your man fails to kill her while we're taking the kid. Plans. Insurance. I have to outthink them and you. Then it turns out they're all as much of an imbecile as you are. It's a wonder I get anything done."

Alan shrank further. Zoe didn't want to feel sorry for him. He was as much at fault, not standing up for himself, but Beatrice was horrible. Theirs was nowhere close to a healthy relationship. They were both crazy, but the woman might actually be certifiable. She thought she could bully her husband into running for president just because she wanted power? Did she think she could bully voters, as well? And the Secret Service, along with the district attorney and the mayor?

Apparently she was intent on getting started with that now.

"It takes money to run a candidacy—you know that. It's why we had to bring the cartel in. Only by laundering their money for a fee did we have the chance for enough cash to fund all my plans. And now it's all ruined." Beatrice let out a bark of frustration. "But no matter. I'll fix it. I will. I can do this."

More than ever, Zoe wanted to unbuckle and jump from the moving car. But the door wouldn't open. The child locks had to be on. From when they'd kidnapped Tyler?

A sob moved up in her chest, and she felt the raw emotion trail down her cheeks in hot wet streams. They were going to take her wherever they wanted to, and they were going to kill her. Then they were going to move on with their lives like nothing was amiss.

Would the Secret Service let them do it? She couldn't imagine Jude letting this go, but Beatrice implied she had powerful connections. Maybe she'd go over Jude's head, and the Secret Service would be forced to back off. Beatrice had said she had everything "in hand." Whatever that meant, it didn't sound good.

"Take a left," Beatrice ordered.

Alan said nothing, but complied, turning left. Another mile closer to their destination.

Where was Jude?

Jude held the door handle while Milsner took the corner. Tyler let out a squeal, which Jude wasn't sure was fear or excitement.

Maybe both. Tyler held his other hand, but all Jude's attention was on the car where Zoe was. Several other vehicles had been between them, but they'd stayed far enough out of sight that neither Alan nor his wife would know they were being followed.

By an entire convoy of federal agents.

Now they'd taken a side street, as Milsner intended to cut them off. The task force was determined to bring them down. It was a point of honor that they apprehend the couple and get Zoe back. For Jude, they said. He'd never appreciated his teammates more than he did today.

"The team is in place," Agent Carnes said through the car speakers.

"Copy that." Milsner hung up the call. They tore down a side street and he pulled up sharply at the corner of the road. Two other SUVs were on the opposite side, the main street between them four lanes of pretty busy traffic.

Jude prayed that with what they were planning, no one else got hurt.

"Wait here." Milsner got out, as did Agent Carnes from the passenger seat. He hadn't needed to say it. Jude wasn't about to let Tyler out of his sight, or put the child in the path of danger again. He trusted the team to save Zoe, and they would.

It wouldn't be long now.

"What are they doing?" Tyler's voice was small, and Jude unbuckled them both to pull the boy to his side.

"Watch."

All the men braced on both sides of the street. The agent from the passenger seat handed a latticed bundle of metal to Milsner. He moved, like a sprinter ready to set off from the starting line.

The agent with him gave a shout Jude couldn't hear, and Milsner threw the bundle in his hands onto the street while he held on to one end.

The spike strip shot out across the asphalt, another coming from the far side of the street. They met in the middle, overlapping. There was nowhere for Alan and Beatrice to go now without driving over the spikes that would wreck their tires and make them unable to continue.

Two seconds later Alan ran over it. Tires popped and the car careened out of sight.

"Come on."

Jude tugged Tyler from the car and kept his hold on the boy's hand as they ran to the corner. Milsner and the other agents surrounded the car. They deflated airbags with their knives and pulled Alan and his wife from the vehicle and hauled them away. Both were injured and out cold, but an ambulance was on its way.

When they were clear, Milsner gave him a nod. Jude and Tyler raced to the car. He opened the back door while the boy stepped from foot to foot. Jude prayed she was okay.

"Mom?"

Jude saw the seat belt and released some of the tension from holding his breath. "She was buckled in."

"She always tells me to."

Jude leaned her back, so she rested her head on the seat. She was out cold. "Zoe?" He checked her over for injuries but couldn't see any new ones. Then he tapped her cheek. "Wake up, beautiful. The sun is just coming up, and there are two men right here who want to see those pretty green eyes of yours."

Her lips parted and a low groan emerged from her throat.

"Zoe?"

Her eyes flickered and she focused on him. Her eyes darted to Tyler, then she relaxed.

"Everything's okay," Jude said. "It's over now."

Zoe let out a breath. "Hi."

Jude smiled. "Hi, yourself." He moved closer to her.

Tyler frowned. "Are you going to kiss?"

He stilled. It wasn't that he'd forgotten Tyler was there, he'd just gotten caught up in Zoe. It was a problem he'd hoped that he'd have to get used to. He glanced at the boy. "Why? You got a problem with it?"

"It's gross."

Zoe's breathy chuckle reached his ears. Jude glanced at her. "I guess we know how he feels about it."

"Just don't do it when I'm watching, okay?" the boy said, far more relaxed now that they knew his mom was all right.

"Not sure I can make that promise, bud." He glanced at Zoe and saw that she was smiling, as well. "Ready to go?"

"Where?"

He picked her up out of the car. Grunted.

"I can walk."

"I know."

"You have a head injury."

"And a big bruise under my vest from where Beatrice shot me. I'm fine."

She didn't look convinced. "Where are we going?"

Jude strode toward Milsner. Alan and Beatrice were likely using the ambulance, given their injuries had been far more extensive. Maybe his colleague would let Jude borrow his vehicle.

Tyler tucked his hand in Jude's biceps as they walked.

"Jude?" Zoe asked.

"Yes, my love?"

Her smile nearly made him trip, but he kept his fcct as she said, "Where are we going?"

"Anywhere you want."

"I love you."

Thankfully Tyler didn't think that was gross.

Jude caught her gaze and replied, "Good. Because I love you, as well."

EPILOGUE

Five months later

Zoe crossed the grass between the church and Jude's tree house. It was a little chilly, but fall had turned the leaves to browns and oranges that she loved. Not to mention Leanne kept baking pumpkin-flavored *everything*. It was the best time of year, as far as Zoe was concerned. Though she did love Christmas.

The closer she got to the tree house, the more she could hear whispering voices coming from inside.

What were they up to?

Lately things had been a little tense. Ever since Jude had found out he was being transferred to the Secret Service office in Washington, DC. It was a huge move, and she was so proud of him. Everyone said he was young to be given this opportunity, as though they were trying to convince her it was a good thing. Why would she not think that?

Still, the worries lingered. He hadn't specifically asked her to go with him, and lately he'd begun to talk about their future in vague terms, though he was always quick to tell her he loved her.

She reached for the lowest rung of the ladder, then bit her lip. If he broke up with her and left, Tyler would be crushed. And, yes, she would be, as well. But Jude was her son's best friend now. She wouldn't be able to bear it if they were torn apart.

The tear escaped before she could call it back.

Jude's face popped out of the doorway. "What's taking so—" He frowned. "Zoe?"

She swiped the tear away, but it was too late. He'd seen it.

"You should come up here."

"Yeah, Mom!" Tyler called from inside. "Get up here!"

Not wanting to disappoint her son, Zoe climbed the ladder. Before she could ask why the inside was full of battery operated Christmas lights when it wasn't even Halloween, Jude touched her cheek. He leaned his face close to hers. It was obvious in the concern on his face that he could see she was sad. "I love you."

Zoe nodded. "I know."

He told her often. So why did that make her sad? She didn't even want to contemplate the fact that he might move to the East Coast and leave her and Tyler here. She loved him so much it would hurt to be apart.

"I want to show you something." His lips curled up into a small smile, and he motioned to the inside of the tree house.

She shuffled through the doorway and folded her legs under her. "What's with the Christmas..." Zoe frowned. "A cake?" Like she hadn't eaten enough cake, cookies and pastries in the past month? He should probably have gotten her a gym membership instead.

"Frosted pumpkin-spice cake." Why was Jude so happy about that?

"Read the words, Mom." Tyler was bouncing.

She glanced at Jude, then leaned forward to read the words iced on the cake.

Will you marry me?

"Say yes!" Her son bounced over and collided with her, knocking her into the man she loved as Tyler said, "Jude wants to be my dad, and I want him to, so you have to say yes!"

Jude's arms went around both of them. "You have to let her answer, Ty."

Zoe's heart filled with so much love it felt like it was going to burst. He wasn't going to leave without her and Tyler and go live some other life of his own? Since Nathan had done that, it had been her biggest fear of this relationship. She shut her eyes as emotion flowed through her. The reassurance of Jude's love for her overwhelmed her, as God's love for her also had.

Zoe started to sob, then groaned because she couldn't stop it. This wasn't how it was supposed to go. She was supposed to say yes, and they would kiss, and instead she was crying.

Jude's arms tightened and Tyler climbed off her lap. "Uh... Mom?"

"Don't mind me. I'm just having a mental breakdown."

Jude's chest shifted with his chuckle.

She glanced up at him. "Are you laughing at me?"

"How about you answer the question?" The gleam in his eyes was beautiful, and she was pleased to be the one who put it there. She wanted to always make him this happy.

"Yes, Jude. I'll marry you."

Tyler squealed, and launched himself at

them. They collapsed in a tangle of limbs and laughter, but Zoe made sure she got a kiss to seal the deal.

* * * * *

If you enjoyed this book, look for the other titles by Lisa Phillips in the SECRET SERVICE AGENTS *miniseries:*

SECURITY DETAIL
HOMEFRONT DEFENDERS
YULETIDE SUSPECT

Available now from Love Inspired Suspense!

Find more great reads at
www.LoveInspired.com

Dear Reader,

Thank you for taking the time to read this book. I so appreciate you, and the fact that it is an investment of your time and money each time I write a story. I hope you were entertained by Zoe and Jude's journey to being a family.

The past hurt Zoe had experienced colored the way she saw the world—especially men—and how she saw the Lord. But God brought her through a journey that enabled her to trust Him and find happiness for her and her son, with Jude. He is a gracious Father who loves to draw us to Himself, and I am thankful for that every day.

If you have any comments or questions, I would love to hear from you! Feel free to email me at lisaphillipsbks@gmail.com and visit my website, where you can sign up for my newsletter: www.authorlisaphillips.com.

Sincerely,
Lisa Phillips

Get 2 Free Books,
Plus 2 Free Gifts—
just for trying the
Reader Service!

Love Inspired

Get 2 Free Books,
Plus 2 Free Gifts —
just for trying the Reader Service!

HARLEQUIN
HEARTWARMING™

HOME on the RANCH

YES! Please send me the **Home on the Ranch Collection** in Larger Print. This collection begins with 3 FREE books and 2 FREE gifts in the first shipment. Along with my 3 free books, I'll also get the next 4 books from the Home on the Ranch Collection, in LARGER PRINT, which I may either return and owe nothing, or keep for the low price of $5.24 U.S./ $5.89 CDN each plus $2.99 for shipping and handling per shipment*. If I decide to continue, about once a month for 8 months I will get 6 or 7 more books, but will only need to pay for 4. That means 2 or 3 books in every shipment will be FREE! If I decide to keep the entire collection, I'll have paid for only 32 books because 19 books are FREE! I understand that accepting the 3 free books and gifts places me under no obligation to buy anything. I can always return a shipment and cancel at any time. My free books and gifts are mine to keep no matter what I decide.

268 HCN 3760 468 HCN 3760

Name   (PLEASE PRINT)

Address   Apt. #

City   State/Prov.   Zip/Postal Code

Signature (if under 18, a parent or guardian must sign)

Mail to the **Reader Service**:
IN U.S.A.: P.O. Box 1867, Buffalo, NY. 14240-1867
IN CANADA: P.O. Box 609, Fort Erie, Ontario L2A 5X3

* Terms and prices subject to change without notice. Prices do not include applicable taxes. Sales tax applicable in NY. Canadian residents will be charged applicable taxes. This offer is limited to one order per household. All orders subject to approval. Credit or debit balances in a customer's account(s) may be offset by any other outstanding balance owed by or to the customer. Please allow 3 to 4 weeks for delivery. Offer available while quantities last. Offer not available to Quebec residents.

HRCBPA18

READERSERVICE.COM

Manage your account online!

- Review your order history
- Manage your payments
- Update your address

> *We've designed the*
> *Reader Service website*
> *just for you.*

Enjoy all the features!

- Discover new series available to you, and read excerpts from any series.
- Respond to mailings and special monthly offers.
- Browse the Bonus Bucks catalog and online-only exculsives.
- Share your feedback.

Visit us at:

ReaderService.com

RS16R